A Place Called Hope

Emma Batten

Emma Batten 2019

All Rights reserved
No part of this publication may be reproduced, stored in a retrieval system, or transmitted in any form or by any means without the prior permission in writing of the publisher, nor be otherwise circulated in any form of binding or cover other than that in which it is published and without a similar condition including this condition being imposed on the subsequent purchaser.

The moral right of the author has been asserted.

First published in Great Britain by Emma Batten

ISBN 978-1-9995820-4-3

Printed and bound in the UK

A catalogue record of this book can be found in the British Library

Edited by Maud Matley

Proofread by Greer Harris

Hope in Ruins cover painting by Phillippa Goddard

www.emmabattenauthor.com

About the Book

The remains of a tiny church stand in the countryside not far from the town of New Romney in Romney Marsh. The church once served a parish known as Hope but by 1589 there were no longer enough people in the area to support it. The vicar moved to St Nicholas, New Romney, and the small church, dedicated to All Saints, was left to go to ruin.

This book tells the fictional tale of families living in this small settlement at the end of the 16th century. Descriptions of their homes and workplaces are entirely from the author's imagination and those of the church come from the limited information available. All characters in the books are fictional and not based on any person living or dead.

Hope is one of several deserted settlements in the area where only the church ruins remain. It is recorded that there were four homes in the parish in 1589.

I am delighted to feature a painting by local artist, Phillippa Goddard, on the front cover. To combine local art with my Romney Marsh fiction makes this book very special to me.

With many thanks to Maud Matley for editing and her never-ending enthusiasm for my writing. To Greer Harris for coming to the rescue as a proofreader and to Sue Parry for additional checks

Also, thanks to all my readers who are giving me so much encouragement and support. I really appreciate every positive comment on social media and personal messages/e-mails which you take the time to send.

This is a second edition of *A Place Called Hope*. It has had a rewrite and new cover since its first publication in 2017.

For Breeze Quinn and Christy Marin, my two friends who were the first to support my author journey when they bought *Secrets of the Shingle* at the time when it was first published in 2016.

Anna's Story
Chapter One

"Well, Odigar, have you any tales to tell?"

We all turned towards Odigar – a tall, gaunt man with hollow cheeks and a shock of iron-grey hair. His skin had the appearance of worn leather, tanned and weather-beaten from daily exposure to the elements. A slight figure belied his strength, for he laboured long, hard hours on the land, doing whatever job suited the season. His company as he worked was a stick, or piece of straw, which he chewed upon relentlessly. I knew him as a man of few words, a curt nod being his usual greeting. Odigar lived a seemingly quiet life with his sister in their cottage of mud and reeds. What stories could he have to interest us?

"There's always tales to tell in a place like Romney Marsh. When the sun goes down and we are in our cosy beds at night there's strange things that happen. I can't say why or how, but there's no other place on earth that attracts the witches and spirits like our Marsh." He spoke quietly and slowly, but everyone's attention was on him. "Aye, I'll tell you a story or two presently, when the young ones have gone."

Midsummer's Eve was a special time for me, and in the year 1584 it was both my fourteenth birthday and a time of celebration for everyone. Every year the

Farley family invited the villagers to enjoy a bonfire party. This birthday was particularly important to me, as I was now considered to be mature enough for my parents to decide I could stay for the whole of the party, rather than leave with the children in the early evening.

It was my favourite time of the year: flat fields of lush grass stretched out in all directions, neither parched by the summer sun nor damp and muddy as they became in winter. The lambs skipped around their mothers, bleating from dawn to dusk. Crops were becoming a beautiful, warm, golden-brown colour and there was hope of a successful harvest. I loved to have the sunshine on my face and to hear the whispering of a gentle summer breeze through the reeds.

Now, having danced madly around the bonfire to the tunes from Old John's whistle, we sat on makeshift benches of planks on bales. Trestle tables were no longer sagging under their burden of the evening's feast and the wooden plates were almost empty. Hauntingly eerie music from the parson's fiddle floated on the evening breeze and mingled with a chorus of cries from the Romney Marsh sheep. I sat on a bench with my close friend, Jessica, talking about nothing in particular and relaxing with a glass of cider in my hand.

The sun began to set, casting brilliant shades of red, orange and yellow over the sky. Across the fields our tiny church, on its raised mound, looked glorious with the dramatic sky beyond it.

"Ah, 'twill be a grand day t'morro'. There can be no doubt with a sky like that." Isaac-the-looker spoke quietly as we gazed with appreciation at the view.

"Time to get the little ones home," his wife, Magota, replied. The baby was asleep in her arms and their oldest child, Nicholas, rested against his mother's legs.

They began to collect their belongings, then thanked Farmer and Mistress Farley for their hospitality. The other families with children reluctantly gathered their brood; the evening had ended for some. Jessica was to take her brother home, while her parents stayed a little longer. "Tell me all about it tomorrow," she whispered.

I promised that I would. Now there was a growing feeling of excitement within me. Here I was, for the first time, another adult at the party. As Mistress Farley offered wine and ale, benches were pulled together closing the gaps that had been left. Nathan, younger son of the Farley family, gestured for me to join him and his brother. I knew Nathan well for, although he was three years older than me, we had shared many years of schooling at the parsonage. With a quick glance at the elder brother, Thomas, I wondered if he minded my company. It was foolish of me, for he turned and gave a welcoming smile.

"Come and sit with us, little Anna," Nathan called.

"Not so little, now my lessons are finished." As I moved towards them they made space for me.

"I remember them well. I was glad to be released from the daily chore."

"I'm sure you have to work harder now."

"I try not to," he whispered, with an eye on his brother.

"My brother is not inclined to work hard." Thomas stood up and I was unnecessarily disappointed to think he was about to leave. He returned with my shawl. "Nathan, you have no manners. Anna will be feeling the cold soon."

The bonfire was beginning to die down. I pulled my shawl around me; there was a chill in the air. The music from the fiddle died out and then Old John – a short, balding man, with a merry smile, who lived alone on the road to Ivychurch – asked the question again: "Well, Odigar, have you any tales to tell?"

"I'm out working the land from dawn to dusk, here and there, meeting all sorts of people." Odigar paused, a faraway look in his eyes. Perhaps he saw the steep, reed-lined ditches he cleared to keep our flat lands drained, or the ruts in our narrow twisting lanes that he filled. "It's a strange old place, there's no two ways about it. When you live in a land that should rightfully be under the sea, then there's going to be strange happenings. Man has meddled with nature and sometimes I wonder if it's right."

"Well, it's our home and I thank God for the Dymchurch Wall, keeping us all safe on our land," Old John added his opinion.

"Aye," Odigar paused to reflect. "I can't imagine living anywhere else, that's a fact. So, I'll join you in thanking the Lord for the Dymchurch Wall, just like those Dymchurch folk do every day of their lives." He took a sip of ale from his tankard, then picked up a stick and began to chew at the end.

"Have you heard of any happenings recently?" Nathan asked.

"There was something I heard. It were over Romney way, Old Romney that is. There were a woman who should have known better than to go out at night. She were a brave woman... I'll say that about her. Well, it were her father, he had a fever... or perchance it was a fall... I can't be sure. It doesn't matter. What I can tell you is that she went out at night to fetch the doctor.

"The mists were rising from the dykes on either side of the road; it were like walking down a tunnel. You know the sort of night I mean: you can't see where you've come from or where you're going. The sheep bleating in the fields makes it feel unsettling. She had her little dog with her. I shouldn't think that dog wanted to be out at night for animals can sense the spirits better than we can. Now, suddenly, the dog froze and would not walk a step further. There were nothing she could do and she needed to get to the doctor. She were concentrating on the dog and when she looked up... it were there. I can't say whether it stepped out of the mists or if it just appeared. That poor woman, she was as petrified as her dog. She knew that could be the end for her..." Odigar paused and seemed intent on chewing his well-worn stick, his steely eyes narrowed as he contemplated the fate of the woman.

The sun was gone now; where it had been, the sky remained lighter, a curious mixture of orange-pink and blue-grey. The church on its low mound was just a silhouette; roadside cottages were barely visible. Into the distance stretched the ditches, or dykes as we call them, which acted as field boundaries. Reeds and stunted trees marked the routes the dykes took as they made their way, turning one way then another, across low-lying countryside. Further away, not even a hint of the hills remained.

The group sat in silence, not tempted to talk, just waiting for the storyteller to continue, apparently content to let him take his time. With the darkness of the night rapidly closing in on us, the atmosphere became more eerie.

"Well, I expect you are wondering what happened next, so I'll tell you. Stood before her was an old hag: silver-grey hair, a great hook nose, and so many layers of clothes covering her. Now, I say 'her' but the woman could not be sure, for the old hag spoke with the deepest of voices."

"Was it a witch?" someone asked.

"A witch? I cannot say. Have you ever seen a witch? Who can say what a witch looks like? Anyway, the woman was asked what her business was, to be out on such a night. She told of her father, fearing now for both his life and her own. It seems that the witch, or whatever it was, thought kindly towards the woman. She were escorted to the doctor's house, and all the way the old hag chanted in a deep voice; the words could not be understood, but it sounded like some terrible spell. The woman was warned to return to her own home as soon as the doctor was ready and not to make a habit of going out at night.

"Well, I think that woman was lucky. She won't leave her home after dusk again, but at least she's here to tell the tale. Her little dog were not so fortunate, so petrified that he had to be carried to the doctor's house and home again. The next day he were found dead in his bed; who can be surprised after what he saw?"

Listening intently to Odigar's tale, I had never realised that he could tell such stories. There had always been rumours of spirits and witches, but in whispers not meant for my ears. Everyone was silent and I watched the glowing embers of the fire. When Thomas tapped my arm, I jumped in surprise.

"Sorry, I didn't mean to startle you. Has Odigar frightened you?"

"Not at all, he tells a good story." Brave words, but the atmosphere was now very chilly and I was glad to be sitting safely between the Farley brothers.

"There are some people who are not so lucky, isn't that so, Odigar?" Old John prompted the storyteller to continue.

"You're right there. None of you should go out at night; there are many that come to a bad end. There is one way to avoid it... listen for them coming, mayhap a muffled beat or a rustle of the reeds. Then cover your face, and if you don't see them... you may be saved. Never take a glance; they'll know, and you'll be sorry.

"Remember that man from St Mary in the Marsh, couldn't speak a sensible word? There was one time when he could read and write, like our Mr Smith and the young folk here. They say that he looked upon a terrible sight, so dazed he were that he never recovered."

"What did he see?" asked Farmer Farley, amidst murmurs of recognition.

"Who knows? I'm no mind reader, am I? He never spoke clear again, but I know that he went out at night for some reason."

The audience remained captive, but it seemed for the moment Odigar was engrossed in the chewing of his stick.

"What of the lookers and the farmers, and the danger to them?" I whispered to Thomas, not wanting to draw attention to myself.

Nathan overheard and repeated my question to Odigar.

"I guess the spirits understand the ways of the Marsh, for where would we be without our sheep? All I can say is that they leave the lookers and farmers alone, as long as they keep their thoughts and eyes off them spirits." Odigar rose from his stool. "Now then, Mistress Farley, do you have a spot more ale for a dry throat? Let's not give the young ones any more nightmares."

We talked for a little longer, before the glowing embers of the bonfire. Odigar's stories filled my thoughts and the atmosphere felt quite magical. No wonder – here I was on my fourteenth birthday and at my first grown-up party, sitting between the handsome Farley brothers, Nathan and Thomas, who had been adults for as long as I could remember. We had feasted, danced and had our minds filled with unnerving tales. I wanted the evening to go on forever, but the women started clearing away the last of the food and the celebrations were over.

My father was a private man who rarely attended a party or any local entertainment, unless it was a religious occasion. He had stayed at home, and so it was just my mother and I who gave our thanks to Farmer and Mistress Farley as we left that evening.

Our home, a single-storey cottage adjoining the forge, was opposite the church in the small village of Hope. I say village, but it was barely that – merely a smattering of dwellings and several of those were uninhabited. There were no places of much interest or importance in the parish, but we were fortunate to be a short distance from the small town of New Romney.

The tiny church, dedicated to All Saints, boasted a tall spire on its square tower and some highly decorative archways. It sat on raised ground, surrounded by a water-filled ditch, and we crossed a causeway from the ancient Saxon track to the churchyard. The sheep used it too and grazed amongst the headstones. In a modest, low stone house, set between the churchyard and the road, the vicar, his sister and her family lived. Their home was in a state of disrepair, as was the church. The only other house of significance was the farm.

I had lived all my life in the tiny community, surrounded on all sides by flat, some would say bleak, countryside. An area of vast skies, looking down upon a patchwork of fields interwoven with reed-lined drainage ditches. Willow trees bent over by the strong, unhindered winds. Hedges of hawthorn with white blossom in spring, red berries in winter.

Hope. I have often thought what a strange name that was for a place. What were those first inhabitants hoping *for*? I wonder if they achieved it. Perhaps they had great ambitions or perhaps they wanted, as most of us do, good health, a comfortable home and a plentiful supply of food. There is no doubt they prayed that the land, recently drained and secured by them, would not return to the sea and that the Dymchurch Wall was strong enough to hold back the spring tides.

Now, on the evening of my birthday, I found myself on the brink of my new adult life. The next day was to be the first in many years when I would not be going to lessons with the parson, along with my friend, Jessica. Instead, I would be thinking of the future, starting with looking for an occupation. What other changes were in front of me: marriage, a new home, children?

Anna's Story
Chapter Two

"Pray tell, Anna Smith, what plans do you have?" My father's words were barked with some force.

"Plans? I'll help Mother clear the table, then perhaps a little darning."

"I speak of your future. You are a young woman, filled with all the knowledge our worthy parson could give in the two hours he sacrificed for you each morning." These words were tinged with some contempt, for Father had little respect for the parson, or for anyone else.

"Aye, Father, my lessons are finished."

It was not uncommon for girls to have no education at all. My father wanted my sister, Eliza, and me to learn to read and write. These skills and some basic arithmetic were taught by the local parson in his home. From my mother, I learnt how to care for the home and family: cooking, sewing, housekeeping and the use of remedies and potions to cure various ailments.

"Well, no doubt your mother has some ideas; she is a sensible woman and can guide you in the right direction. Be sure to read passages from the Bible daily and do not indulge in idle gossip."

He turned, picked up a news pamphlet and his attention was withdrawn as quickly as it had been focused on me. It may well have been the longest speech I had ever heard from my father. Now he sat reading intently, with his thick, dark eyebrows drawn together in a frown. Every crease in his hands, arms, face and neck was lined with the dirt from the forge, which was his own business and livelihood.

Mother and I exchanged glances and, by mutual, silent agreement, we began to clear the supper dishes. As we tidied and washed up, few words were spoken; we were relieved when he left the table to make himself comfortable in his chair by the fire. We were then able to speak freely. Whether it was about our household tasks or local news, Father did not want to be bothered by our chatter.

He was a reclusive, bitter man who appreciated none of what he had and dwelt on all that he had lost. Until the age of fourteen he had led a different life, brought up in the town of Maidstone, the son of a wealthy businessman. Father was well-educated and had expected to live a comfortable life in that town. However, his father dragged the family into disrepute by gambling heavily which caused great financial problems. My father was sent to live with his mother's cousin as a temporary arrangement. He found the countryside rather dull but, having spent his childhood occupied with study, he now found the new skill of working with iron an interesting diversion.

But, after the busy town of Maidstone, the small village of Hope, set among the bleak, flat land of Romney Marsh, was not a place he had ever intended to settle. However, he was never asked to return to Maidstone; the business had failed and the family destitute. Now, he was no longer enjoying a holiday in Hope but was destined to stay here. By the age of twenty, he had inherited the forge and within another year my mother was pregnant. Father was no longer in a position to make any great changes to his life. He became a man who gained no pleasure from his home or family: a silent depressive figure. Henry

Smith he became, for it seemed he inherited the name with the forge and had no choice but to accept his fate.

An unexpected rap on the door was followed by its being flung open and slamming against the kitchen wall.

"Come on, Bess, stop that snivelling. Pick her up, William." Eliza, my sister, burst into the room and settled herself down on the bench, elbows on the table. "Surprised to see us, I expect?"

"It's not like you to come calling in the evening." Mother held out her arms to Bess, who was happily transferred from her father to grandmother. "Is everything well?"

"It's her teeth, I can't abide another night of her crying," Eliza replied.

"We wondered if you had some medicine, perhaps herbs to soothe her?" William asked.

"What happened to the pot of calendula I gave you last week?" Bess' plump arms were wrapped around my mother's neck and she stroked the tousled fair hair. The baby began to relax as she was gently rocked from side to side.

"I left it open and the damp got in; all mouldy it was." Eliza shrugged her shoulders, dark eyes roaming around the kitchen, her lips set in the familiar, discontented pout. "The woman next door was no help, said I should go to the apothecary and she wouldn't lend me anything else."

"I do have a little more, but you could grow a few herbs in your patch of land." Mother reached for a clay pot and transferred some dried daisies into a piece of cloth. "Now, take this but do remember to use that little pot I gave you last time."

Eliza took the package. "I see you've got a bit of fruit pie over there, I keep meaning to make one but..."

"Take it, it's no trouble for me to make another." Mother pushed the dish across the table towards Eliza.

"We could grow a few herbs," William agreed with my mother. "I thought of getting a few chickens, too."

"And who would clean up all the mess? Nay, I'm not cleaning up after a load of dirty squawking birds." The decision was made and Eliza's attention fell upon me. "Finished your lessons, Anna? Never did me any good; it's all the same when you've got a family and a home to look after, knowing your letters won't make any difference. Still, you won't know about that for a while. Six years younger than me, you don't know how your life will change."

"It helped you get the work in a shop, and there are worse jobs than being out of the wind and rain serving customers all day." Eliza had done well for herself, I thought. She had a lovely husband, too: you wouldn't find William wasting his wages in the tavern or gambling their money away.

"It's fair enough for you to say, but try being with all those powders and potions all day, they gave me such a headache. Now, it's this one here that gives me the headaches." Eliza gave a nod in the direction of her daughter, asleep and content in her grandmother's arms. At only twenty years old, the bloom of youth was long gone, her skin sallow. My sister's hair, once fair like my own, was dull and lank, secured with a piece of string.

"If you've got what you came for, then best get the child home and give the rest of us some peace," Father muttered.

"I'll carry her." William took Bess, making sure that her head was comfortable on his shoulder and the blanket wrapped securely around her.

William had such a pleasant, agreeable

character. As an odd job man, living and working in New Romney, he had met Eliza when she worked in the apothecary. Eliza saw in William a man who could be dominated and moulded into a suitable husband. She ensured they were engaged to be married in no time.

Before she was married, Eliza had arranged for William to have an apprenticeship with my father. Once married they lived in New Romney and William walked to Hope every day, to work alongside my father. Father and daughter were as cheerless as each other; how William must have looked forward to that half an hour walk every day, free from wife and employer! He could not linger, for both would be quick to criticise if he were late.

On that warm, summer's evening, my sister and her family walked home to their two-room cottage. I was alone with my parents. Mother and I did a little darning and talked occasionally but mostly we were left to our own thoughts.

It was surprising my mother had not been affected by my father's ill humour. Somehow she had remained cheerful and seemed contented with her life; Mother accepted things as they were. If my father had been able to do that, I believe he would have been a happier man. Mother was a slim woman with pale golden hair and smudged freckles across her nose and cheeks, always busy and never complaining. She and I were similar in looks and temperament, as were my father and sister. I wondered how it was that a warm, happy, person could be attracted by a quiet, reclusive man. Sometimes I asked my mother, but always got the same answer.

"He was a handsome young man when he first arrived here, different from others. He didn't come from the Marsh, you know."

"Was he content then?"

"Aye, he thought he was going home, back to Maidstone. He said that I could go with him. Then it all changed and, with our Eliza on the way, it was too late for your father to better himself. He had the forge and it gave us a decent living, but it was not what he wanted for himself or his family."

"Mother, must he always be so miserable? There is no fun in this house once he comes in for his supper."

"Hush, Anna, he is your father and deserves some respect. He is a good man and has had a hard life. We are fortunate he provides so well for us."

Perhaps my father would have been happier if there had been a son for him to fulfil his ambitions through. A son to educate and give opportunities. I did not speak of this to my mother as there had been two boys born before me; both died shortly after birth.

Mother put down her darning. "We'll ask in the apothecary's tomorrow, to see if there is any work available," she said. "Eliza always liked to go there, despite her complaints! You could learn a little about the remedies, which would be useful if you decide to help me with my work."

My mother worked as the local midwife, as had her mother and grandmother before her. There were not many babies born in our village, so she would go to Romney or Ivychurch when needed. We had the luxury of our own pony named Cobweb. He lived in the field beyond our cottage and allowed her to travel quickly to the neighbouring villages when needed.

"I did not expect a daughter of mine to have to go out to work," Father muttered, not lifting his eyes from his book.

"I don't mind, Father," I replied. "It will keep me busy and I'll enjoy meeting people."

"It is a shame when a girl wants to go to work to

amuse herself. There is little enough to occupy anyone on this miserable Marsh. Why, even our good Queen Elizabeth would not soil her pretty feet by travelling through this accursed place." Father's voice grew louder as he warmed to this common subject.

I was about to reply when mother silenced me with a frown and a nod. The meaning was clear: Let him say his piece; he is your father and we must respect his opinions.

"I wish I had never set foot on the Romney Marsh; I expected better for my family." Father glanced up at us and then turned back to his book. The subject was closed.

The idea of working in the apothecary appealed to me and I went with my mother to ask if there was a position available. I was offered employment six days a week, with a half-day on Wednesday and Saturday. It was a little daunting, a completely new way of life, spending my days with different people and learning new tasks. However, I looked forward to it and, within two days of securing the job, I was up early and ready for a day's work in the town.

On the first morning, I was offered a ride into the town on the farm cart with Mistress Farley. She was going to sell farm produce on a market stall. It was a treat to travel by in this way and her cheerful conversation helped me to forget my nerves. We were soon in New Romney and, for the first time, I stepped down from the cart to start my life as a working woman.

There had been a time, hundreds of years ago, when New Romney was a thriving coastal town. It had a duty to the King to provide ships to be used in battle. A wide estuary had deep moorings for large ships and they came from all over the world to trade here. Following great storms, the river mouth became blocked and the river took an easier route, out to the sea at Rye. Attempts to revive the harbour had failed and the prosperity of the town declined.

It was the only town I knew and was able to hold a great deal of interest for me. Compared to Hope, New Romney had a large population and I loved to watch the people go about their daily business. Father may have preferred me to stay at home but I was glad of the opportunity to see a little more of life.

The main street was lined with buildings of various sizes and ages. Most had a shop facing on to the street with living quarters behind. Newer buildings boasted one or two floors above the store, in which the owners and their families lived in some comfort. Many of the buildings had stood for decades and were improved or extended when it was possible to do so.

It was fascinating to watch the morning activity as shopkeepers prepared for the day. Some displayed their wares on benches outside the shop. The butcher hung animal carcasses from hooks so they swayed above our heads. The smell of raw meat was unappealing and with it came the flies swarming around their tasty feast. Worse than that was the squealing of animals as they were killed to order, ensuring the meat was at its most fresh.

The smell of tanned leather was better, and I always had a nod from the cheerful shoemaker sitting in the doorway of his small shop. But the most tempting aroma of all came from the bakery, especially in the early morning when the bread was still warm from the oven. Then there was the apothecary, which had the sweet scents of perfumes and lotions combined with the unusual smells of medication, powders and potions.

One of the largest shops was the general store run by the Blackstock family. It had an assortment of foods and household goods. There was also the barber's shop, the printer's, the ironmonger's and the draper's. Market stalls sold fresh fruit and vegetables, dairy products and a variety of home-made foods.

Beyond the main street were the houses of the townspeople. Some were made of stone or had a sturdy timber frame, filled with mud and straw. Chimneys had been added over the last few decades. There were small yards with sheds for storage and space for poultry, a pig and a small vegetable plot. Other homes were no more than shacks, with no glass in the small windows, no chimney and often just one room.

In Cannon Street and Church Road were the larger and more comfortable houses of the local gentry, or more prosperous traders. The whole town was overlooked by the church of St Nicholas with its sturdy square tower. It was here that much of the town's business was conducted, including local councils and courts.

The sea was now half a mile away from the church walls that it had once lapped against; it had retreated over the centuries. I often walked to the beach of sand and shingle to buy the fish sold by local fishermen. Their boats came in on the tide and were pulled up on to the beach until the next tide took them out to sea again. The waters were shallow, unsuitable for larger vessels which could have brought prosperity to the town.

I found I enjoyed my new routines, although the working days were longer than I was used to. My time spent at work depended on the season; we opened later and closed earlier during the dark winter days. My employers were friendly and patient as I learnt new skills. Mr Peake was a small, slim man with a pointed nose too large for his face. He leaned forward attentively as customers told of their ailments, and nodded knowingly. He had a great understanding of the wide variety of illnesses people suffered from and advised which medicines were suitable. Glazed jars stored the traditional herbal remedies alongside new drugs that came from our country's trade with the East: senna, aloes and *nux vomica*. Customers could barely afford the doctor's fee and took the apothecary's advice for common problems such as coughs, colds, dysentery or rheumatism.

Mistress Peake was a busy woman, with several children to look after. She was more often in her home at the back but helped occasionally in the shop. Standing a head taller than her husband she was called upon to reach the highest shelves and came with goodwill, perhaps holding a baby on her slim hip or frantically trying to push back her thick golden curls that forever escaped her headscarf. She showed me all the sweets, lotions, perfumes and fancy goods which were popular as presents. A great favourite was a perfume made from marjoram. To keep the skin soft, we sold beeswax and sesame oil, and for the eyes there were Kohl pencils. This was the area of the shop I preferred, but it was the drugs and remedies which were most sought after.

I met new people and learnt new skills. I found that I was quite content with my life. It was not long before my friend, Jessica, celebrated her thirteenth birthday. Her family decided that she was old enough to start work and she was offered a position in the drapery owned by a member of her family. We were able to walk to town and back together and compare the experiences of our new lives.

Anna's Story
Chapter Three

I always looked forward to Easter time. It came after several months of cold wet weather which hindered us in many ways. Now our homes became less damp, the roads were easier to travel on and there was a greater variety of food upon our table. With the hedgerows full of white hawthorn blossom, lambs in the fields and renewed growth of grass, trees and reeds, the Marsh became a less dreary place to be.

Even the very poor tried to provide their families with something new to wear. In some cases this meant adjusting someone else's clothes they had outgrown or discarded. Some added new trimmings to an old skirt or patches on the knees of breeches or to elbows of a tunic. Those who could afford it bought new material to be made into clothes, either by themselves or a local woman. I had saved up a little money to enable me to buy some cloth. Mother and I had chosen material from the draper's shop in New Romney. It was a mid-blue colour and we added silk trimmings; I had new hair clips to complement it. Our neighbour, Mrs Browning, had made me a skirt and bodice from the new linen cloth.

Children enjoyed the custom of decorating eggs and I welcomed the chance to help them. Jessica and I spent a pleasant Saturday afternoon at the parson's home doing this before setting off to deliver them throughout the village.

That evening my mother and I carefully pressed our new clothes. We welcomed the heat from the fire, as the evenings were still chilly. Outside the mist had risen from the ditches and even my father's sombre mood would not encourage me to leave the comfort of our warm room. Father put bricks beside the fire and, once they were warmed through, my mother wrapped them in cloth and placed them in our beds.

That night it took me a long time to fall asleep as I drew the bedclothes tightly around me, trying to warm myself. Then I heard the sound of muffled footsteps. Perhaps some sheep had strayed from the fields, or the parson was making a late night call. Whatever the reason was, I dared not look from the window for an answer.

Easter morning came and, while the mist still hung in the air and the dew was heavy on the grass, I went to let Cobweb out of his stable. There was no welcoming whinny or comforting horsey smell. There was no pony in either the stable or in the field. Neither was there any sign that Cobweb had escaped; both stable door and field gate were securely bolted.

"Cobweb's gone!" I rushed back to the house to tell my parents.

"Don't fret, Anna. He won't have gone far. The bolt must have not been pulled across," Mother replied, without turning from the pan of porridge she was stirring methodically. "We'll look for him later, or most likely he'll make his own way home."

"I heard footsteps last night. I should have looked – I could have stopped him being taken."

"You know better than that, Anna," Father snapped, and the very fact that he spoke meant his words were of importance. "No girl of mine goes out at night or looks to see if it's a witch or a pony causing a disturbance. If it were to be a spirit of the

Marsh you could come to regret your curiosity." Father pulled on his cloak, then picked up some bread and cheese. "I'll find your pony, for you never know when a baby will choose to come and your mother may need him."

"There, Anna, that was good of him," Mother commented, but stirred the unwanted porridge with less enthusiasm as we watched his departure.

I paced up and down, unable to concentrate upon anything until I knew Cobweb was safely back in his stable. Mother encouraged me to have a little breakfast; it lay like clay in my stomach. Stepping out into the fresh air, I looked up and down the road then across the fields. There was no sign of either my father or the grey pony. Returning home to the morning chores, I collected eggs from the chickens and water from the well. In my room the new outfit hung on a hook; it would give me no pleasure until the pony came home.

An hour passed before there was a knock at our door. My mother answered it and found Thomas Farley standing there, looking uncomfortable in his Sunday suit rather than his old farming clothes. He ran a hand through his hair and smiled, but not his usual smile which reached his eyes.

"Is Mr Smith at home?"

"No, he went out to look for the pony," Mother told him.

Thomas stepped into the cottage and stood for a moment before he spoke. "I'm so sorry to be the one to bring you bad news. Isaac was out early morning checking on the lambs, and as he passed Paternoster sewer he thought he saw a ewe in trouble. He went to take a look and saw... he saw it was your pretty little pony. He was too late to be any help. Looks as if he fell, trying to jump the dyke."

"Oh, the poor thing! What can he have been up

to? He must have broken out." Mother's words came out quickly, and then she faltered for she was fond of the animal, too.

"Are you sure it's too late?" I asked quietly.

"I'm sorry, Anna." He looked down at me and I was glad that if this news had to be brought to us then it was done by this kind, young farmer.

Thomas left us to our grief. I watched him walk along the road, where he met my father and they spoke for a few minutes.

"Well, that is bad luck," were the only words my father said, as he came back into the house.

The church bells rang out but brought no joy. Neither did I appreciate the first outing in my Easter skirt and bodice. I felt numb and confused. The stable door and field gate were bolted; how could Cobweb have escaped? The small congregation sang as enthusiastically as ever; I opened and closed my mouth in time to the music, but barely a whisper came from my lips. As hard as I tried to concentrate on the service, all I heard was the same unanswered question repeated in my head. How had this happened?

The service was over. We left the church and I moved away from my neighbours who gathered to talk. Through my misery I noticed that my father was talking to Odigar and Old John. It was unusual for him to make conversation with anyone and it seemed they were arguing. My father suddenly walked away, leaving the other men to continue talking in a calmer manner. At the time I had no energy to consider this, it was much later that I remembered the scene and understood.

Someone approached me. It was Thomas. He did not speak immediately, but it was a comfort to have his company. He seemed to understand that I didn't want to talk about Cobweb; there was nothing else to say about him. Here was a man who could be trusted to do the best he could in any situation.

"We have two orphan lambs," he said. "Twins, born three days ago. Would you like to help me and give them a bottle? They need a lot of care."

I murmured agreement and told Mother where I was going. As we walked along the track to the farm, Thomas didn't make much conversation. He offered a diversion, but didn't pretend that all was well.

The lambs were in a straw-filled enclosure within the large barn. They rose on unstable legs; even at three days old they knew when to expect food. Thomas suggested that I keep them company rather than face the busy farmhouse kitchen. He went to warm some milk and soon returned, even thinking to bring a rug to save my new clothes from the dirt.

We each fed an eager lamb some creamy milk. They sucked enthusiastically on rags dipped into a bowl of the warm liquid. As orphans, they were dependent upon us and it was good to feel needed. Milk bowls were soon empty and the satisfied lambs curled up to sleep.

"We've been lucky this year; we only lost the one ewe," Thomas commented.

"They must take a lot of looking after."

"They do, but they give us pleasure too, and they soon grow up." Thomas hesitated, and then said: "Come again tomorrow, if you like."

"I'd love to. Thank you for taking care of me, it was kind of you." I stood up reluctantly, "I'd better go now."

In the cottage adjoining the forge, everything continued as usual. The kitchen was warm and filled with the aroma of food cooking. Mother was preparing a meal of salted beef with carrots, swede and bread. I took plates and spoons from the oak dresser and placed them on the well-scrubbed, plain wooden table. Mother spooned the meat and vegetables on to the plates. I cut slices of bread to soak up the gravy and fill our stomachs.

My father ate in silence as he usually did. Mother and I would often talk a little, but were not inclined to that day. I wanted to ask the question which played on my mind, but was wary of my father's temper.

"Father," I spoke with caution, "when I went to the stable, the door was bolted. Cobweb could not have left by his own doing."

"What other explanation could there be?" My father asked the question without raising his eyes from his plate.

"I don't know, perhaps you could..."

"It's done now, Anna. Don't meddle with things you don't understand."

"More bread, Henry?" My mother started cutting another slice. The subject was closed.

After work the next day I went to the farm to collect our milk, cheese and butter. Both Mistress Farley and her daughter, Ellen, were in the dairy. Their heads were close, as Mistress Farley encouraged the girl to master the technique of patting the butter into shape; auburn curls were touching as they tried to escape the restraints of their caps. Turning at the sound of my steps, they smiled. With a generous smattering of freckles covering their noses and cheeks, there could be no mistaking them as mother and daughter.

"Good day," I greeted them.

"Nice to see you, Anna. Would you like to feed the lambs again?" Mistress Farley did not wait for a reply and continued: "Ellen, go and call Thomas, he's with Isaac in the near field."

"Thank you, I'd like to. And please could I have some cheese and butter, as well as the milk?" I handed my milk jug and basket to Mistress Farley.

"I'll get that ready for you." Then her face sobered for a moment as she added: "I am sorry to hear your news; he was a handsome pony."

"He was, Mistress Farley."

Ellen returned and beckoned me to go to the farmhouse kitchen with her. The milk needed heating and was ready when Thomas walked in. He took the milk and I followed him to the barn. It was good to be amongst the comforting smells of hay and animal feed. The lambs stood up with enthusiasm, bleating for their milk, and were soon suckling.

"How are you?" Thomas asked.

"I'm fine; it helps to come here and be occupied. I don't understand what happened to Cobweb... how he got out. Father... well, he... I can't really talk to him about it." How could I explain how confusing it was? Everyone knew what a sullen man my father was, but it was best left unsaid.

We spoke of other things instead. Thomas talked about how he enjoyed farming the land that had been in his family for generations. He spoke of his paternal grandfather who had died a few years before and how he had brought plenty of money into the farm, enabling the building of a fine brick farmhouse. He asked how I enjoyed my work at the apothecary's and enquired after my sister and her child. All too soon, it was time to leave with an invitation to visit the lambs again after church the following Sunday.

Over the next few weeks, we welcomed the lighter mornings and evenings. Grass in the fields became lush; sheep grew plump on the rich pasture. I got pleasure from seeing the orphan lambs grow in strength, and soon they were able to join the others in the fields. The countryside became drier, the mists less frequent, the roads less muddy. Reeds grew up on the banks of the dykes and danced in the wind.

I still thought of Cobweb, of him dying alone with no one to help him. Sometimes at night I would dream that I heard his footsteps and he was coming home. Then I woke to the realisation that it *was* just a dream and I had to suffer the intensity of my loss again. Sometimes the dream and reality became muddled; I was sure I could still hear the footsteps when I woke.

One morning, when the dew was still thick on the ground, I carefully picked out the best route across the garden to the hen-coop. My eyes were on the rough grass and earth, not looking out towards the fields. When I heard the whinny, clear and shrill, it brought back the sadness. When I heard it again I looked beyond the hen-coop to see a pony. She was a sturdy bay mare, whom I had never seen before.

"Mother! Mother!" I was calling before I reached the house.

"In here, Anna." She was tending the fire and looked up with concern showing in her face. "Don't tell me there's been a fox in with the chickens, not after your father strengthened the fence."

"What's this about a fox?" Father slammed down his bowl and got up from the table.

"The chickens are fine. There's a pony in the field."

"Oh, the pony. Someone thought it would be needed... that your mother would find her useful." Father left for the forge, leaving questions unanswered.

"Well, Anna, I can't say I'm sorry." Mother picked up a shawl as we went to inspect the new arrival. "It will be handy having her nearby; a baby won't wait if it's time to come."

The pony was pleased to see us and nuzzled at our hands. She seemed to be gentle and stood calmly whilst we talked to her and wondered what she would have to say, if she could tell us about her life. We decided to call her Bonnie and I knew that, in time, I would grow fond of her, but she would never replace Cobweb in my affections.

Anna's Story
Chapter Four

Midsummer's Eve was soon with us again. It marked my fifteenth birthday. The weather had been consistently hot for several weeks. By mid-morning, I felt it was warmer than ever before; how I longed to discard my woollen bodice and skirt just as the men in the fields threw off their shirts and tunics. The air seemed to shimmer above the land and the distant hills, marking the edge of Romney Marsh, were masked by the heat haze.

I walked home from work with Jessica and her father; the road was dusty with deep cracks emerging. A cart carrying fresh fish, just brought in on the high tide, passed us. The horses trotted briskly; they had to reach Ashford whilst the catch was at its best. Dust was sprayed over us as they passed; seagulls circling above mocked our misfortune with their cries.

"This dust gets everywhere." Jessica shook out her long skirt and stamped her boots on the grass verge.

"The mud is worse," I commented, trying to look on the bright side.

"I don't think this heat will last much longer. There's a storm brewing and it wouldn't surprise me if it came before the day was over." Jessica's father pointed to the north-east. "The sky looks to be darkening towards Ashford way."

We looked in that direction and nodded our agreement.

"It would be a shame if it spoiled the bonfire." I had been excited all day with the prospect of feasting, dancing and storytelling ahead of me.

"We can still have a good time and the roads will be less dusty tomorrow." Mr Browning was right of course; we did need some rain.

By the time an hour had passed, the sky was a curious mixture of pale blue and dark purple. Looking one way, it was a pleasant summer's evening. In the other direction the atmosphere was menacing. As time passed, the dark purple became the dominant colour in the sky.

Later, Mother and I met Jessica and her family on the way to the farm. The community gathered as usual for the annual Midsummer party. We walked into the farmyard to be greeted by Mistress Farley, who beckoned us towards a small barn.

"We've set the food in here for this evening. The good weather won't hold; Martin says it will be raining before long. Still, a bit of rain won't spoil our fun!"

We placed our share of the feast on a trestle table. The parson and his widowed sister, Dorothy, were talking with neighbours John and Mary:

"Let's hope that the young ones are not frightened by his tales tonight," Dorothy said, giving a nod in the direction of Odigar.

"He certainly tells a dramatic story," Mary added.

"I've suggested that a nice reading from the Bible may be more..." but the parson gave a snort of laughter, causing his sister to stop mid-flow.

"Let them have some fun tonight and on Sunday they shall hear from the Bible," the parson said.

Jessica and I chose to enjoy the bonfire whilst the weather held. We walked around the corner of the barn to find the blaze was being provoked by Nathan, wielding a long branch. Thomas watched carefully, ensuring no stray embers touched the parched grass. That was how it was with them: Nathan enjoying the moment, Thomas taking care that all was well. They waved a welcome.

Magota watched her young children playing. She was only about five or six years older than me but her life was completely different. Her days were filled with caring for her family. That night it was her husband's turn to be out in the fields, keeping an eye on the sheep and their lambs. The baby, Zachary, was over a year old now; his solid legs carried him as he eagerly followed his brother. He kept his balance surprisingly well on the rough ground but then he fell and his face crumbled in despair as he turned to his mother.

"I wonder what the future holds for us," Jessica frowned, as we watched the young children with their mother.

"Marriage, children. The same as everyone else. I expect."

"You're fifteen today, perhaps your father is thinking of a husband for you?"

"I don't think he spends much time thinking about me."

"At least I don't have to worry about that yet," Jessica said as she sat down on a bench. "But I do look forward to being able to stay up to hear the storyteller. You'll tell me his tales, Anna?"

I promised I would. Her brother, James, approached us, eagerly demanding that we play a game with the children. We agreed to join in with their version of skittles, throwing a ball at some pieces of wood, carefully balanced on the rough ground. There was no more chance to talk privately. It was fun but before long those first large, slow-falling raindrops halted the game. Then it was truly raining and we ran for cover, and to the food in the barn.

It was warm in there and the air was stuffy, thick with dust particles from straw and hay. Once the rain clouds covered the sun, it was also quite dark. Candles were held in deep bowls, limiting the light they gave and lessening the risk of causing a fire.

These discomforts did not spoil our joy of the occasion. People were glad of a change from their usual routines, to talk with their neighbours and watch the young children play. There was plenty of good food to eat and ale or wine to drink. A merry tune was played on a whistle; men tapped their feet and women clapped their hands in time to the music.

Jessica and I collected a selection of food, then paused, looking for a suitable place to sit. Nathan, close to the entrance doors, nodded towards some space on the benches. Thomas joined him with a jug of wine intended for us to share. We were pleased to sit with them, for not only were they good company, they had secured a place near the doorway, where a refreshing breeze blew through.

Children became sleepy once they had eaten and played. Those with young ones prepared to leave. The children complained of the unfairness, but Nicholas and Zachary were almost asleep and Brice, the parson's nephew, was cuddled up against his mother.

Once again, I was left with the adults to enjoy the rest of the evening. Everyone seemed relaxed and not tempted to move from their seats. They talked in an idle manner of local affairs. I wondered if there was to be any storytelling that night.

"It's been unusually hot for June, wouldn't you say, Farmer?" Old John asked, as he reclined on the straw, a mug of ale in his hand.

Farmer Farley nodded in agreement. "Oh aye, I

wasn't surprised to see it break. The land needs a drop of rain; another week or so of this weather and it would have been parched."

"The Spirits of the Marsh will care for you, if you keep them happy." Odigar spoke in his quiet way, but at once all eyes were on him. "Our good farmer here must know to mind his own business and leave them a little gift on occasion."

"Odigar, don't you scare the women with your tales of spirits." Nathan poured himself some wine and then offered the jug to Thomas and me. I thought for a moment that the time had gone and there would be no more talk of Marsh Phantoms.

"Well, it's best they understand the ways of the Marsh." Odigar's voice was low, ensuring everyone sat still in order to hear. He was not to be deterred from whatever he had to say. Plucking a piece of straw from the bale, he tore it to shreds, eyes narrowing as if he brooded on some dark secret. In the half-light his face appeared leaner than ever, with great shadows in the hollows under his cheeks.

There was silence in the barn as we waited. The children had gone home, our stomachs were full, rain beat down on the roof. We relaxed on our seats of hay and old sacking. Thomas touched my arm lightly, causing me to jump. "Are you frightened?"

"Not at all." I held my head high and straightened my back.

Odigar knew all our attention was on him, yet he looked at none of us directly. He was waiting, so as to give more drama to his tale and the atmosphere grew a little more chilly. Clearing his throat, he took a sip of ale and began: "Like I said, the farmers need to keep the Spirits of the Marsh happy. So many things can happen to a farmer that could cause poverty to his family and hunger for his neighbours. There were a farmer over Brenzett way that suffered badly for spiting the folk of the night."

"What do you mean by that?" Jessica's father asked.

"Well, Clement, I'll tell you all about this farmer. He met an old man, dressed in clothes that were not familiar to him and his skin... it were as pale as the moon. This man, or maybe he were a spirit, he told the farmer that he was to leave his stable unlocked at night. The other thing he asked for was a few wool-packs; they were for a good cause.

"Now, before you all start asking questions, I'll tell you that I don't know any more than I've told you. That old man disappeared into the mists once he had delivered his message. The farmer were not inclined to take heed and made extra sure that the farm was secure that night.

"The weather had been dry and sunny for weeks. The farmers were all busy gathering their harvests. It was no different for this farmer: the hay and other crops had dried out in the fields, then were taken by cart for storing in the great barn. I bet the farmer was relieved when the work was done, for that night there were a great storm, just as we have now."

Odigar was silent for a few seconds. We listened to the rain beating down and the crack of distant thunder. A flash of lightning lit up some faces and threw shadows across others. We could all imagine how pleased that farmer was to be warm and dry in his home. I shivered violently; the evening had grown cold. Thomas placed my woollen shawl on my shoulders.

"That night a bolt of lightning hit his barn. With all that dry hay and straw, the fire soon took and within an hour or so all his crops were lost. There was nothing he could do to save it. As he watched the barn burn he saw the pale-faced man standing there, just looking. He only saw him for a few seconds...

then he were gone." Odigar paused to let us all picture the dramatic scene.

"Now then Odigar, you are frightening the young ones with your tales. You should know better." It was an elderly neighbour who spoke. She was a sour-looking woman, critical of others.

"Mother, shall I take you home?" her son asked; he was a quiet man and did not want the party spoilt.

"No, John, I shall stay here and enjoy a little more wine." There was a great deal of fuss as people moved aside to enable her to fill her cup, then she took care to make herself comfortable again. It seemed that the mood of the evening was to be broken. She was not going to let the matter lie: "As I was saying, Odigar should take care not to be giving people nightmares."

"The children are in bed; those who are here are old enough to become wise to the ways of the Marsh. One day they may be glad they listened to my warnings." Odigar said no more and seemed intent on chewing a piece of straw. He knew the audience would be his again... if he waited.

The elderly woman sipped at her wine. She could not resist one more comment, "It's disrespectful to be telling stories, while his sister is barely cold in her grave. What would Avice think?"

She spoke more to herself than anyone else, but Odigar had sharp hearing and heard the words.

"Now, I am glad you mentioned Avice, God rest her soul, for there was a something that happened to her before she passed away." All attention was back on Odigar and the elderly woman tutted her disapproval. "She had a dream just before she died, so vivid she half-believed it happened. Avice dreamt that a tall, thin person came to her bedside and stood there just looking at her. His hair was all over the place and his skin was pale, his eyes sat in great dark sockets. I said he were tall and he was, so tall that he had to stoop or his head would be going through the roof.

"At last he spoke in a whisper and he warned her that no living soul should be out past nightfall on the first of July. It was a night for witches, ghosts and things we could not imagine. They would not take kindly to intruders."

"And was it a dream?" Farmer Farley asked.

"I can't answer that. I was downstairs clearing away the supper dishes, with Avice unable to stir from her bed. It's up to you all to believe what you will." Odigar raised his tankard and smiled broadly. "Time for some ale; all this talking is thirsty work!"

Odigar made it clear that his entertaining was done for the evening. The villagers moved into groups rather than sitting together in a circle. They watched the storm from the door of the barn, commenting as to whether or not the rainfall was less intense. Others spoke of parish matters with the parson, or of farming with the host. My own mother was speaking with Jessica's mother; I guessed from their gestures that they were discussing dressmaking.

I sat, listening to the soothing rhythm of rain upon the roof. Odigar's tales certainly enthralled his audience; I wondered where he got his information from. Were we meant to believe that the Marsh at night came alive with mystical figures, or was it merely intended as amusement? If it was just entertainment, then why did each story hold a warning? I puzzled over the content of those from this evening and others I had heard before. There was no doubt this was a clear warning: it was unsafe to go out at night. Was it time to question these rules, I wondered? I needed time to watch, listen and try to make sense of the mystery.

"Anna, you're quiet. Not scared by Odigar's tales I

hope?" Nathan's voice had a hint of amusement to it.

"Not at all. He tells a good story." I knew Nathan could not be trusted with the seeds of an idea growing in my mind.

"Well, if you need anyone to look after you..."

"Then she will know better than to turn to my little brother," Thomas added. "I'm pleased you enjoyed yourself, especially as it's your birthday."

"I did." I turned to smile at Thomas. Looking up at him I realised that he was the person I could talk to about almost anything.

Anna's Story
Chapter Five

There was one person whose opinion of the Marsh Spirits interested me. My father's contempt for the area in which we lived was clear for all to see. Surely he would give little credit to tales of Marsh phantoms. He was an educated man and I felt he must have some comments to make upon the subject.

That evening, as Mother ladled pottage, I cut slices of fresh bread. My attention was not on the task; I was wondering how to broach the subject. Father came to the table, poured himself a tankard of ale and settled down to eat.

"Father, thank you for allowing me to go to the Midsummer party," I spoke with hesitance.

"You enjoyed it then?" he replied, without taking his eyes from the plate.

"Aye, very much."

"Good."

It was not an encouraging start.

"Father... it surprises me to hear so much of the terrible things that happen on the Marsh at night. Was it the same where you lived as a boy?"

"Of course not," he snapped. "Maidstone is a civilised town. It's only in a place like the Romney Marsh that such demons live."

"It's not just a story then?"

"A story? Have I not told you all your life what a grim and thankless place this is to live?" He rose from the table and leant forwards, arms outstretched and hands gripping the table. His eyes were dark with anger and his brows knitted together. "Perhaps the girl should not be hearing these tales if they give her nightmares."

"Father, I'm fine." I should not have raised the subject.

"Anna, there is no need to worry yourself about these matters. Your needlework needs completing and I was wondering if you would look in the draper's to see if there are any ribbons to suit my Sunday bodice." My mother clearly wanted to change the subject.

"Of course. I'll look tomorrow."

I busied myself with clearing the table, hoping that my countenance was one of someone who had no other interests than matching ribbons. I found some fruit, which would go nicely with cream from the local farm, then served my parents and myself. We settled down to eat in silence, but could not relax until my father was seated in his chair by the fire, his fury directed at religious pamphlets, rather than me. My parents might have thought the subject was closed but I still wondered about the truth of Odigar's tales.

The following day was Saturday. I worked a half-day and was glad of the opportunity to have time to myself in the afternoon. It took half an hour to walk home from the town. Wandering along, I watched the lambs playing in the fields and the farm labourers at work. There was a slight breeze that caused ripples on the water-filled ditches and the reeds to whisper quietly amongst themselves. It was a pleasant day, but my true reason for lingering was so as to make plans for the night of the first of July. The more I thought about the strange happenings on the Marsh, the more certain I became that I wanted to discover the truth for myself.

"Would you like a ride home?"

I jumped upon hearing a cart behind me. It was a relief to see it was Thomas driving the heavy farm horse. He slowed down and stopped beside me then leant down, his strong arm outstretched, offering me his hand.

I took his hand and stepped up into the cart and thanked him. The horse plodded on slowly. I was still thinking of my plan and remembered that I had wanted to discuss it with Thomas, sure that I could trust him with my thoughts. He had been so kind to me when Cobweb died and I felt that we were good friends now.

"Thomas, there is something important I want to ask you. You may think I am being foolish..."

"I would never think that, Anna."

"It's about Midsummer's Eve."

"Were you frightened? It's just a story; people enjoy it."

"No. It's just that I wonder... I wonder why it is that Odigar always warns us not to go out at night? It's not just Odigar, is it? Everyone says that we shouldn't, or even look from our windows." I looked at Thomas, ready to note his reaction.

Thomas commanded the horse to stop; it was grateful for the chance to graze on the lush grass at the roadside. He turned to look at me, brown eyes meeting my cool grey ones. I saw confusion and concern in his face.

"That's the Romney Marsh; you know the way it is, Anna. Strange things do happen here at night."

"That's what I am told, but is it true?"

"I don't know what you mean." Thomas looked puzzled.

"Odigar warned us not to go out at night on the first of July. He warned us against it. Why would he do that?"

"That's the message he had from Avice," he reminded me.

"No, I believe that there is another reason. There is something going on, I don't know what but Odigar wants to make sure no one sees it. He's not the only one, I know it."

Thomas shook his head slowly and sighed. He seemed to be undecided about what to say.

"Anna, have you spoken of this to anyone else?"

"No, not even Jessica."

"Thank God for that." His body relaxed and there was a slight smile, a return of the warmth I usually saw in his face.

"I have decided to go out on that night and see for myself." I watched him closely for a reaction.

"Anna, no!" There was fear in his voice and a return of the tension in his body.

"I'll be careful; I'll go around the churchyard and then wait by the roadside."

Thomas took my hands, shocking me with the intensity of his concern. "Please Anna, you can't go out at night. It's... they are, they..." He held my hands even tighter. At last he made a decision and spoke clearly: "Anna, there are things happening on the Marsh at night, and people making sure no one knows of them. Just accept it. You are too special to be mixed up in things you do not understand. It's not safe."

"So I was right to wonder and perhaps one day I'll learn the truth?"

"You will, Anna; you have a curious mind and are sure to discover the answers."

Thomas let go of my hands. He smiled at me, a look of relief on his face. The reins were gathered and the horse began to walk on.

"I had better get you home." His voice was deep

and filled with emotion.

A small knot of guilt settled in my stomach; I had not changed my plans.

A strong wind blew across the countryside on the night of the first of July. Tree branches swayed, shedding their load of raindrops from the earlier showers. There was the occasional groan of an open gate swinging under the pressure of the gale. Water in the ditches gurgled and the reeds rustled. Sheep bleated their complaints; the Marsh had become an eerie place.

I had expected to be moving around in a silent night-time world, alert to the sound of any other person who was about. Instead it seemed each noise was magnified and sounds that went unheard during the day were now causing me to jump, to look around with fear.

The sky was mainly overcast, clouds constantly racing across the face of the moon. I strained my eyes to search for any other person and saw no one. Moving forward carefully, I felt my way until reaching the shelter of the church walls. There was no turning back, although I longed to race down the path, up the road and back to the safety of my bed.

I rested for a few minutes against the rough stone wall of the church; it was a relief to be out of the wind for a moment. There was only one more field to cross; not as easy as it seemed when the countryside was riddled with dykes. However, the crossing was found easily and I moved cautiously around the edge of the field before reaching my hide: a group of hawthorn trees beside the edge of the field, overlooking the lane. Finally, I settled down on the long grass; it was uncomfortable, but I felt well hidden.

Minutes dragged and I was soon wondering

whether I had been foolish to come out at night. Perhaps there was nothing to see, or had I chosen the wrong place to wait? I decided to remain where I was. Then the footsteps came – or was it my imagination? All the noises of the night seemed unfamiliar. Perhaps it was simply a rabbit or a fox going about its nocturnal activities. But the steps came closer, the wet road causing water to splash up as the person walked swiftly by. He wore a long cloak and a hat and I didn't see his face as he passed. My heart raced in fear and anticipation, but there was something familiar about the way the person carried himself and I suddenly realised it was Old John.

I was not surprised to see his destination was Odigar's cottage. He entered without knocking. Within minutes two figures appeared. Both wore long cloaks and hats and when the moonlight shone down for a moment, I saw faces unlike any I knew. One was mostly dark, the features changed by streaks of grey-black across the cheeks and around the eyes. The other was paler, but the eyes were in deep dark pits, perhaps achieved by rings of charcoal on the skin.

The two phantoms of the Marsh did not speak; they scurried across the road then stepped down on to the bank of the dyke. Then they moved more slowly, hindered by the reeds and uneven banks. Within minutes I could only see their shoulders and heads drifting along, just about level with the road.

I followed, only moving forward when they were almost out of sight. Finally the figures rose out of the dyke and I froze in fear of being discovered. Without looking back they crossed the farm track and entered the next field. I continued until I came to the farm track and decided not to go any further.

There seemed to be a group of people in the field. I could hear the sounds of horses pulling at grass, their leather bridles creaking, and then a gentle whinny. Clouds moved away from the moon and the scene was lit up: a group of figures, perhaps another five men and about ten horses. The horses were laden with packs and had hoods over their faces. The darkness and distance meant that the men were unrecognisable to me. Dressed in layers of tatty clothes with hoods and scarves, their faces a mixture of dark and light, they soothed the horses and checked the packs were secure. Two people carried a plank of wood and I wondered why.

Then the moon was concealed by a cloud, leaving the group barely visible, which was infuriating. When its light shone, they were moving away. One of the sinister figures, perhaps Old John or Odigar, separated himself and returned in the direction he had come from.

There was no time to retrace my steps. He would notice me and must be much more adept at moving swiftly on the rough ground. I decided to move up the farm track and into the vegetable plot of the looker's cottage. I would be well concealed there. As I rounded the corner of the cottage, a hand went over my mouth and I was pulled into the shelter of some bushes.

My assailant had a firm grip; my back was against his chest, I could not see him but knew him to be a strong man, tall and broad. Inside my head Odigar's warnings were clear: I had seen too much and my life was not safe. I feared the worst as the man bent down to whisper in my ear.

"Don't struggle – it's Thomas." He loosened his grip and removed his hand from my mouth.

And now my heart raced with excitement. To be pulled into the arms of this young farmer, to have his arms tight around me. Then the fear returned: was Thomas involved with these night-time activities? Would he do me some harm? He must have felt me tense and held me a little less firmly. I turned to look up at him, still held in the circle of his arms, and could see no malice in his face. Our eyes were locked for several seconds.

"Why did you have to do it?" he asked.

"I was curious." There was no other explanation.

"You are foolish; I shudder to think what would have happened if you were caught."

"I *was* caught."

"I had to make sure you were safe; I couldn't sleep for worrying you may be out here and in danger." Then, as if suddenly aware that he held me close, Thomas stepped away from me. I felt more vulnerable; his arms had been comforting. "They're gone now, for an hour at least. We can go somewhere to talk, but you must be home before they return." He took my hand and guided me past the back of the lookers' houses and into the farmyard. We went into the barn.

"What did you see?" Thomas gestured for me to sit on a crate.

"Men. I don't know who. Horses and packs of something; they were in the field."

It was warm and dry in the barn, but outside the wind still howled. Branches of a tree scraped against the wall; there was a rhythmic beat of an open gate or loose piece of wood knocking on something. Mice or rats scattered when we entered the barn, but I knew they were still there.

"I'll tell you, Anna. Then you leave it be, go home and leave the men to their business." He stood up and went to the barn doorway, looking out into the yard, then turned back to me.

"There's not always much money to be made in farming, even on this rich pasture. The price of wool is low, but we could do better if we sold it overseas. The government doesn't want this and has imposed such high taxes that it doesn't make it worthwhile. So our Romney Marsh wool, and even wool from further inland, is smuggled out of the country at night."

"That's what the horses carried?"

"Aye. That's the explanation for the stories of witches and ghosts: to make sure the land is deserted and the smugglers pass unhindered. They disguise themselves to scare anyone who does see them and to hide their identity if they are caught."

"Does Odigar arrange all of this?"

"Odigar? What do you know of Odigar?"

"Nothing, only that I saw him and Old John leaving his cottage."

"No, he merely passes on messages and helps with the delivery of wool. There is someone else who has organised the operation: the collection of wool, which horses are to be used, where to meet. He'll collect the money from the French tonight when they receive the wool-bales on the beach. The same person will pay the owlers, our name for smugglers, for their work and the farmers for their wool."

"Does this person have contacts abroad? How do they know when to do the smuggling?"

"I can't answer that. I believe that there is someone else who does it, not a local man. Maybe someone as far away as Canterbury or Maidstone. I can tell you what you saw here tonight was only a small part of it. The person who has organised this has arranged for many of our local communities to do the same tonight."

I thought about all that Thomas had told me, trying to understand how the whole operation worked. It was clear quite a few of my neighbours were involved and the extra money allowed them to live in a little more comfort than would otherwise be possible.

"I see why Odigar tells such tales now, although it

seems a shame that people have to live in fear of the Marsh spirits."

"They also benefit from a few luxuries," he reminded me. "Now, we must get you home. I'll take you back across the fields. The area should be clear of owlers at the moment; they'll be on the beaches handing over the wool-packs."

Thomas gestured for me to follow across the edge of the yard and into the fields. Our path depended on the lay-out of the dykes; they were vital to keep the land drained but hindered a direct route. So this was why the smugglers carried a plank, to enable them to cross a narrow dyke at the most convenient place.

The moonlight was limited and I concentrated on my footing on the rough ground which was wet and slippery in places. The wind still blew strongly, whistling through the trees and animal noises continued to startle me. But, with Thomas' hand in mine, nothing was as terrifying as it had been when I was alone.

"Thomas," I whispered, pulling on his hand. A niggling doubt had come into my head. I tried to push it away, but it worried me.

"Anna, we can talk more about this another time, I promise."

"It's just one thing." He stopped and turned towards me. I felt encouraged to continue: "Are you an owler?"

"No, Anna," he said. "I'm a farmer and we provide the wool. So, I'm not innocent, but that's how things are around here and it provides money for the farm. We're paid well. Now, let's get you home."

We reached the roadside opposite the forge.

"I'll leave you now; be careful," Thomas warned. "If you see anyone, say that you went to check on the pony, say you were worried that he may have got out, like Cobweb. Now go, Anna. I must get home." He took my hand briefly and looked down into my face, his frown deep and eyes unsure. "Come to the farm tomorrow afternoon, we can talk then. Come to see the lambs. Now go." Then he was gone. I crept across the road and within minutes I was back home. But sleep eluded me; my heart raced as I relived the events of the night from the safety of my bed.

Anna's Story
Chapter Six

I was awake early the next morning, despite my lack of rest. Summer sunshine streamed through the gaps in my curtains. The wind had died away and the land was peaceful. Looking out of my window, up and down the road, everything was as usual. Who would have thought that such a seemingly quiet place would become alive with activity after nightfall?

As I prepared for the day, most of my thoughts were with Thomas. He had shown himself to be a true friend, risking his own life to ensure I was safe. Who knows what foolish thing I may have done next if he had not found me?

How strange to be sitting in the familiar kitchen of my home, my parents nearby and engrossed in their own thoughts and tasks for the morning. It was a normal day; at least it appeared to be the same as any other. But now I knew the secret, the secret of the Marsh people, my life would never be quite the same again. I tried to eat my porridge so as not to arouse my mother's concern, but it lay heavy in my stomach. It was hard to continue as normal when my mind was filled with last night's revelations and my guilt about Thomas.

On the way to work, I met Jessica and we walked together, passing Odigar's cottage. Was he inside, counting his profits from last night's work? Probably more money than he made in a week or even a month of labouring on the land. Or was he still in his bed, catching up on his sleep? Did he feel any remorse that he told such tales, causing his neighbours to be terrified of leaving their homes after dark?

Opposite Odigar's cottage was the field where I had witnessed the beginning of last night's dark deeds. I wondered what had happened next; had the owlers made it safely across the dykes and fields to the coast? How were the wool-packs transferred to the foreign ship? How many people and horses from the Marsh had been involved? The whole plot must be carefully arranged so everything ran smoothly. The more I pondered over the little I knew, the more I wondered about the many details. My curiosity was far from satisfied.

"Anna, what's on your mind?" Jessica interrupted my chain of thoughts.

"I'm fine. Why do you ask?" I forced myself to concentrate on the moment.

"I have been talking to you, but I don't believe you heard one word."

"It was such a windy night; I had problems sleeping. My window frame was rattling." I smiled briefly, hoping to give the impression that all was well.

"If you're sure…?" Jessica's eyes narrowed as she contemplated my answer and accepted it.

"Mother would like some tonic from the apothecary, so I'll be seeing you later. It's James, he…" Jessica continued to chatter about various matters. I tried to concentrate on her words, but afterwards I could not remember any of her conversation.

We parted once we reached the main street in the town. It was bustling as shopkeepers prepared for the day, some displaying their goods on benches outside their shops. Housewives were waiting to buy the freshest food at the earliest opportunity. Farmers' wives were bringing their produce into the shops or to sell on their stalls.

The last thing I wanted to do was to go to work that morning, but it had to be done. As I tidied, stocked up the shelves and served customers, I found myself irritated by the demands and struggled to keep my mind on the tasks. If only I was at home and able to make any excuse to walk along the lane to the farm and check Thomas had arrived home safely.

"Anything wrong, Anna?"

"You're not looking yourself today, Anna."

"You do look a little pale dear, perhaps you need a tonic?"

Several times during the day I was asked if I was well and my answer became well worn: "Just a little tired… it was the wind last night, keeping me awake."

I asked again what they wanted or faltered over adding the costs. The customers agreed that it had been a windy night and I must be sure to get to bed early that evening.

It was not until mid-afternoon that I spotted Mistress Farley a little way along the street. I strained to look through the window and picked up a cloth to clean the small panes of dusty glass. She was talking to a local woman, her manner appeared to be as usual and I was reassured that all was well at the farm.

Later, feeling rather self-conscious, I walked up the track to the farmhouse. Was there some change in me that showed I had secrets to hide? Would people wonder if my interest in the lambs was genuine or were there other reasons why I was spending time with Thomas? I was too unworldly to consider that if anyone had wondered at my interest in Thomas, they would have thought my motives to be romantic rather than a curiosity in the local smuggling. The memories of the owlers' activities were foremost in my mind and to me it seemed amazing that people could not guess my secret just by looking at me. The knowledge I had gained made me feel as if I was as guilty as those men.

"Come in, Anna dear. Now, where is that son of mine?" Mistress Farley opened the door wide and beckoned for me to come into the farmhouse kitchen. Her smile was sunny and she did not question my visit but shook up a cushion and offered me a seat. "Ellen, will you find your brother, please?"

I sat down on a bench and looked around the room. The walls were plain white, painted plaster with few ornaments, some framed tapestries and amateur paintings. There was a dresser displaying plates and bowls, its cupboards full of cooking utensils. The large brick fireplace dominated one wall, the fire creating a great deal of heat on a warm summer's day. A joint of meat was roasting on a spit. At the sturdy wooden table in the centre of the room, Mistress Farley was preparing vegetables. The table top was well worn, having been used by generations of farmers' wives. Dried herbs hung in bunches from hooks on the wall. In one corner of the room was a door, leading to the cool pantry where food was stored. It was a welcoming room, filled with mouth-watering aromas and cheerful personalities.

"Would you like a glass of milk?" Mistress Farley asked.

"Thank you. That would be lovely."

"Then you're off to see the lambs?"

"Aye. Thomas says they've grown a lot. I'm so glad they survived without their mother."

"And how is your mother? Is she expecting to deliver any babies soon?"

We continued to talk; she was interested in local affairs and spoke kindly of everyone. Her hands were busy chopping onions and carrots, then extracting peas from pods. I was impressed at the speed at which she worked; everything was swept into pans to be cooked later.

"Good day, Anna. Has Mother been looking after you?" Thomas entered the room, his clothes dusty but neatly patched, a hat protecting him from the worst of the summer heat. He seemed to be at ease with himself, showing none of the tension I felt.

"It's nice to have a chat," his mother replied before I could. "Now off you go and if you see that brother of yours, don't forget to remind him that we'll be needing more wood for the fire."

"Very well, Mother."

"Goodbye Mistress Farley, thank you for the milk."

We walked across the farmyard and then set off across the flat fields. It was a beautiful day, immense blue skies with only the smallest wisps of cloud. The grass was lush after recent rainfall. Fringing the dykes, reeds barely moved in the slightest of breezes. It was a pleasure to be away from the village; I could avoid my neighbours and the suspicion that they may be involved with the smuggling.

"Now we can speak in private." Thomas strode out, shoulders back, at ease on the rough ground.

"There is so much to ask, I don't know where to begin."

"I'll always spare the time for you; we can talk again another time." He turned and smiled ruefully as he watched my attempts to cope with a long skirt caught against long tufts of grass.

"Shall we find the lambs first? Will you know which ones they are?"

Thomas assured me that he knew which lambs

were the ones reared by his family. There they were in the next field, skipping around as enthusiastically as their playmates. I worried to see them near the edge of a dyke, then tottering down the steep, uneven slope to the water's edge. It seemed that at any moment they might lose their balance and tumble. Thomas tried to reassure me that they were more sure-footed than they appeared. Then, exhausted by the activity, the lambs eventually folded their awkward legs beneath them and dozed in the sunshine.

We sat in the shade of one of the few trees, leaning against the trunk, legs stretched out, idly twisting long pieces of grass in our fingers.

"I can't stop thinking about the smuggling," I admitted to Thomas, "wondering how it works and who is involved. To think all this happens at night, while innocent people sleep."

"It's not happening every day, or even every week. And don't forget these people bring a little more money and luxuries to their families. Life is hard and we deserve some pleasure."

"Are many people involved?"

Thomas turned to look straight into my face. Struggling with his conscience and how much he should tell me, he sighed, gave a half-smile and shook his head slightly.

"I only tell you this because I trust you to keep it to yourself. It is better you know the truth than cause trouble for yourself by being too inquisitive."

"I wouldn't betray your trust, Thomas. You've been a good friend to me," I replied.

"I hope I always will be. The smuggling of wool is quite a trade on the Romney Marsh, but can only be done in the months after the sheep are shorn. The French have things to offer us, too, goods that are so highly taxed here that common folk can't afford them.

"It works the same way. The owlers are bringing wine, cloth and leather into the country. Someone organises which horses are to be used, when and where they are to meet. They are dressed up as you saw before and make their way to the landing place on a beach. The tubs of wine and the cloth wrapped up in oilskins are brought ashore. The horses are loaded up and the cargo is taken some place where it can be safely stored."

"What happens next? Is it sold locally?"

"No, the owlers are given a cask of wine or a bale of cloth for their work. They are satisfied with this payment; they can't afford that quality with their wages. The next night some of them are busy again: they take the goods off the Marsh and meet up with others who take it to the big towns or cities for it to be sold. The owlers' work is done, until next time."

"It must take a lot of organising."

"I should think it does. Remember, there is a local man who is overseeing the whole operation here on the Marsh; he is in contact with the person who has arranged everything. I expect he passes on the money and probably has a few extra benefits for his trouble."

"Do you know who this man is?"

"No, I have a few ideas, but he may not come from this parish or even the next. I doubt many of the owlers know his identity as he would want to protect himself."

I sat thinking about everything Thomas had told me, occasionally asking another question so as to get everything correct in my mind. Clearly it must take a lot of organising to ensure all the owlers knew when and where to meet, that the horses were collected and returned safely and the French were met at the right time. I thought how exciting it would be to watch the cargo being unloaded on the beach.

"Thomas, have you ever seen it happen?" I asked with assumed innocence, twisting wild flowers into my long pale hair, which lay loose over my shoulders.

"Seen the smuggling?"

"On the beaches. Have you seen them bringing in the cargo?"

"No. I told you I'm not involved."

Thomas had been leaning in a relaxed manner against the tree trunk, legs outstretched, eyes half-closed in the bright sunshine. He suddenly sat bolt upright, the movement causing me to jump.

"No, Anna, *no*! Just leave it at that; it is a dangerous thing to be curious about."

"I was just..."

"I care too much about you to see you get yourself into trouble."

"But, I just wanted to look one last time... to go to the beach and see it all."

"It's dangerous."

"Not if you were there; you would take care of me." I smiled and he returned the smile, flattered by my trust in him. I was encouraged to continue. "How interesting it would be, to see how it all worked. It wouldn't be difficult for me to get out at night."

"It would be dangerous."

"Perhaps not, if I had someone with me, someone who knew the countryside better and could guide me around the dykes, finding the safest way." I looked into his face, not understanding then that for a young man it was hard to resist the pleas of a young woman, who sat in the summer sunshine with flowers entwined in her hair.

"Foolish as well."

"If I could just see the owlers one more time then I would be satisfied and be sensible forever after."

"I would hate to think of you in danger." Thomas picked up and snapped the dead twigs that lay on the ground.

"You would keep me out of danger, please say you will?" Looking into his face, I saw the confusion there.

"It's better if I'm there to keep an eye on you, rather than worry that you have gone alone." Thomas began to relent.

"Of course it would, and it would only be the once." I felt triumphant.

"This can happen only once and we must be careful. No one else is to know about it; idle chatter could leave us in a great deal of danger." His voice had a sharp edge to it, "You'll have to be patient; it may be several weeks until I hear of another operation and I must not arouse suspicion by asking too many questions."

"Of course. I have spoken of this to no one and will wait until it suits you." I could afford to be generous now he had agreed to my plan! "I'll even wait until after harvest time when you are a little less busy."

"How thoughtful!" he replied with a grin, and made no more objections.

It was a beautiful day to sit relaxing in the sunshine enjoying Thomas' company. However, I had come to see the lambs and couldn't take up too much of his time. We returned to the farm and parted with promises from Thomas that he would let me know when he heard some news.

Throughout the summer, the long, hot days continued as usual – dusty roads, green fields turning to golden-brown, a greater variety of fresh foods and the occasional opportunity to go for a walk or a picnic on a Sunday. We lived a simple life, the highlights being religious festivals and times when a travelling show or pedlars came to New Romney. Several months could go by with nothing out of the ordinary happening.

In that time, I became less shocked by Thomas' revelations and accepted that the owlers certainly made our lives a little more comfortable. My curiosity had not waned though, and I still waited for the time when he would tell me that we could witness the smugglers at work. I found myself looking at what people wore: trying to spot the materials that had come from abroad, wrapped in oilskins and brought to us by sea. I looked for clues to tell me which of my neighbours were involved and few were exempt from my suspicion.

During those summer months and into September I saw very little of Thomas. Perhaps he would be in the distance working in the fields, or in the farmyard when I collected our dairy produce. The only time I could be sure of seeing him was at either the morning or evening church service on a Sunday. We would sometimes exchange a few words afterwards.

Then there was no opportunity to give more than a quick greeting, a smile or a nod. During the first weeks of autumn, our congregation expanded for a month or so, as the large church in Ivychurch was having repairs and some of its worshippers joined us. It seemed that the Farley family were on good terms with another farmer from there and the two families spoke together before and after the church service.

The one who encouraged most attention was a girl who was perhaps a year or two older than me. Her name was Abigail and she attached herself to Thomas from the time the family entered the churchyard until the time they left. Her brothers were of a similar age to Thomas and Nathan; they made a merry gathering.

They were present for the Harvest Festival. It was a joyful occasion, with the church decorated and the songs reflecting our thanks for the bountiful harvest.

Afterwards, I caught Thomas' eye and he moved away from his group.

"How are you keeping?" Thomas smiled, but I sensed a lack of the usual warmth from him.

"I'm well, thank you. It was a good harvest, you must be pleased."

"It will make the winter months easier for us all." The words were polite, typical of those exchanged between neighbours.

"It was a good service; the hymns were enjoyable," I said, wishing that we could speak at ease about more interesting matters.

"Our neighbours from Ivychurch increase our numbers and make it a merrier occasion."

And prevent us from speaking to each other as they take your attention away from me. My thoughts were bitter and best left unsaid. Instead my words were as suitable as ever: "It is good to see our church full when our own community is so small."

"It makes a pleasant change." Then just before Thomas turned away, he lowered his voice for his final words: "Next Friday, meet me here. eleven o'clock... dress as they do, I'll bring charcoal for our faces."

I nodded my agreement, trying to keep the excitement and anticipation from showing. As he walked away, I saw that Abigail was watching and soon engaged his attention again.

Nathan spoke to me as well that day. He joined Jessica and me as we left the churchyard. He asked how we enjoyed our jobs. As usual, his manner was friendly, as if life was easy and quite a joke. Then he asked if we had any young men, perhaps a prospective husband? I found this bothersome; he shouldn't have spoken in that way.

"Perhaps wedding bells will ring soon," Nathan commented with a grin. He looked towards Thomas and Abigail. "I expect to hear an announcement any day!"

He gave us another smile and was gone; in a few long strides he had joined his family and friends.

"I pity the woman who marries *him*," declared Jessica before changing the subject.

My happiness after speaking with Thomas and nervous expectation were gone. My heart and stomach felt heavy at the thought of losing a good companion in Thomas.

Anna's Story
Chapter Seven

As the days passed, my anticipation mounted and finally the long-awaited Friday evening came. Throughout the day I tried to suppress my excitement as I thought about the prospect of learning more about smuggling. It was a struggle to eat a supper of fish and vegetables while the nerves in my stomach were doing somersaults, but I needed a good meal inside me if I was to be walking to the coast and back before morning.

"Eat up, girl; there are plenty who would enjoy a nourishing meal. Did you not see those poor souls at the harbour waiting for the scraps?" Father roared his disapproval.

"I did, Father, and I'm grateful to have good food." How foolish of me to allow the attention to be upon myself.

"I'm sure you are, Anna." Mother cut bread and offered it.

The hours dragged that evening. I tried to concentrate on my needlework, but it was not easy to settle to a task. At last the time came when I could go to my room, as if I were going to bed. I lifted my mattress to pull out sacking sewn into a cape, boy's breeches and a large floppy hat. With the charcoal, our features would be well disguised.

It was not long before I heard footsteps and listened carefully to be sure that both parents were in their bedroom. Then I waited a while longer, until I assumed that they would be asleep, then a little longer to be sure. I carefully opened my bedroom door; the hinges had been recently oiled and shouldn't creak. Cautiously, I moved into the kitchen... and waited. No one had heard me.

With the hat over my head and cloak reaching the ground, I opened the front door and, after making sure that the road was deserted, I hurried across it. Stars shone brightly in the clear night sky, the crescent moon was high above. The breeze was slight, barely moving the rushes or the leaves on the trees. This still, moon-lit countryside was a world away from the windswept, eerie night when I first discovered the owlers' secret.

"Good evening." Thomas was waiting for me, concealed in the shadows of the church porch.

Silently, I smiled my greeting. Thomas produced some charcoal and leant down to gently smudge some around my eye sockets, his fingertips rough on the thin skin. Then he applied some to his own face and his eyes appeared to be sunken. He took a cap, which had been tucked under his belt of rope and placed it on his head, pulling it low over his forehead. We stood back and surveyed each other, grinning with surprise and approval. Then, with a slight frown, Thomas removed my hat and reached out, catching all my hair behind my neck. It tingled at the touch of his fingers; twisting it he piled it on top of my head, securing it within the hat.

"We must hide your pretty golden locks."

"Of course."

"Let's go, we've quite a walk ahead of us."

He led the way from the churchyard, around a field and to the farmyard. Stepping carefully between tools, animal dung and rough ground, we crept towards the edge of the farm buildings. Then Thomas took my hand and guided me through the gap in the barns and we were pushing through the long grass behind the dairy, with a narrow dyke to our right.

"I cleared this a little earlier," he told me. "We mustn't draw attention to ourselves and it makes a good hiding place." We were hidden from the farm by the dairy and the reeds concealed us from the owlers who were to meet in the field on the other side of the ditch. He pointed to some sacking on the ground. "We may have to wait a while before they're ready to leave and I thought it best to have something for us to sit on."

We sat close together, our backs against the rough stone wall. I was thankful for the sacking, which was placed on a pile of reeds, but after a while the stones and bumps on the ground began to make their presence known. After half an hour or more, we could hear the creaking of horses' bridles, the occasional whinny and the sound of them snatching at grass. This was accompanied by various noises as the group met up and prepared for the night's work. Peeping through the reeds, we could see shapes of the animals and men moving, but it was too dark to make out any detail. Once the wool-packs were strapped on, the owlers would journey towards the coast. We would then follow; until that time we could only sit waiting in silence

I looked up at Thomas, my good friend. I had no other close friendship with a man. Shop keepers and their assistants, fishermen and farmers, I saw plenty of young men. But for me, none compared to Thomas Farley. The unusual basis for our friendship had brought us closer than would normally be possible.

"Are you comfortable?" Thomas nudged me.

"I'm fine." My reply was whispered.

What a strange situation to be in with a young man, and probably my last chance to be alone with

Thomas. Nathan had suggested that his brother had intentions towards the farmer's daughter, Abigail. The ideal choice as a wife for him I thought, with a pang of regret.

Thomas looked at me and our eyes met for several seconds. I felt my heart lurch uncomfortably. What was he thinking? Did he compare her with me? Perhaps he was thankful that her spirit was not as free and that her curiosity would not lead her into a situation such as this. A man wanted a wife who was subdued and competent in all household tasks, with the strength to bear healthy children.

"I can't believe that you talked me into this." Thomas spoke quietly, his voice deep and serious as he disturbed my thoughts. He shook his head and half smiled. "If you change your mind, it would be the sensible thing to do."

"We've come this far, but it is the last time. I promise."

"It must be; it's too dangerous." He reached for my hand.

"For both of us, I know that. After tonight, I'll forget all about it."

"Good. I can't bear to think of you becoming any more involved in all this. You're..." Thomas let go of my hand and leant forward to look through the reeds at the scene of activity in the field. "They're moving off now – in a few minutes we can follow."

I nodded in agreement and waited, left to wonder what I was, according to Thomas. He didn't return to the subject and I didn't like to ask; I might not like the answer. There was no more time to ponder over his opinion of me as he stood up and motioned for me to follow him.

The plan was to follow the owlers from the neighbouring fields and at times we had to move quickly in order to keep up. They carried planks to enable them to cross the narrow dykes at whatever point suited them. We had to go out of our way to use the usual entrances and exits. It was frustrating that we didn't know where the smugglers were going; it would have been easier if we had been able to plan the route beforehand.

As we neared New Romney, the men turned direction towards the north-east and headed straight towards us. We found that we were ahead of them rather than following. Stepping down into the steep, unstable side of the dyke, we scurried along. Once we came to a group of bushes, where we were able to wait for them to pass by. We were again left to use the longer route as they crossed the dyke and took their portable bridges with them.

It was fortunate that the fields were known to Thomas; they were farmed by his family and he had known them all his life. He confidently found his way around them, although hindered by the darkness. We frequently stumbled on the rough ground, but kept moving forward at a good pace. Eventually, we reached a road that the owlers chose to use rather than the fields. At first we were close to them, separated by the dyke, which ran between road and farm land. The lack of obstacles enabled them to travel faster than us, and the distance between us increased. Clutching each other's hands, we had to move faster over ground that became less familiar to Thomas.

This road was on the outskirts of the town and had clusters of cottages at the roadside. The owlers clearly had the confidence and experience to risk moving through an inhabited area. One of them had separated from the party and went on ahead, probably on the lookout for any person who should not be out at night. I knew anyone he met was in danger; Odigar's tales were still fresh in my mind.

We came upon a dyke that could not be crossed. It was frustrating but an inevitable challenge when choosing to travel across country. The road that the owlers followed turned towards the coast. We turned in the opposite direction and had to walk half the length of a field before we found a way of crossing the ditch.

"How shall we catch up with them now?" I asked Thomas.

"We can tell where they are heading, so there shouldn't be a problem." Thomas tightened his grip on my hand as we crossed the narrow bridge over the dyke. "Can you go a little faster or are you tired?"

"I'm fine; I don't want to lose them."

With the dim moonlight showing us the way, we continued. When we reached the road again we paused, straining our eyes for a sign of the men, then spotting some movement to the east.

"This way." Thomas spoke quickly and motioned for me to keep more closely to the bushes and reeds the hid us from their view. "Keep a watch out."

Once we reached the coast road, it seemed clear our journey was almost over. More owlers were gathered on the beach, just a little further along the road in an area known as Jesson. Although not far away, they soon moved out of view as they made their way down the sloping sands. We would have to go nearer if we were to see the action.

"That's it for us, we can't risk crossing the road." Thomas paused but, sensing my disappointment, he said: "Well…. we could cross here and from the bank we'll see them clear enough, but you'll have to lie flat on the shingle."

I nodded my agreement and we scurried across the coast road. The smell of salt water was strong, clinging to the pebbles and debris thrown up by the tide. We lay flat on the shingle bank, relying on the ridges to keep us concealed. The tide was midway down the beach; the wind was slight.

I knew we were there to watch the French unload a cargo and collect our wool. But that knowledge did not lessen my surprise when I saw it really was happening. "The French are here, see how close their ship is!" I breathed.

The foreign vessel was sailing as close to the beach as it dared. A rowing boat was tied alongside and wool-packs were being passed across. Another boat was being pulled up on to the sand and, before it had beached, the owlers were eagerly wading into the sea to collect casks and bags. The goods were swiftly passed on to others who carried them up the beach and secured them to the horses.

A couple of men seemed to stand back, occasionally going to assist, mainly ensuring that everything ran as arranged. The owlers were clearly experienced; each seemed to know his job and the operation appeared to run smoothly. As the last of the casks were delivered to the beach, the rowing boat returned to its ship. The men climbed the rope ladders and were ready for the voyage home. The boat turned; slowly and silently it moved away. On the beach, loads were made safe and the owlers started the journey inland.

"We'd best move quickly... we need to get ahead or it could be a long night for us; who knows where they might go?" Thomas whispered with urgency.

Crouching as low as we could, we ran across the shingle and back on to the roadside. We were in front of them.

"We've made it before them, now run." Thomas grabbed my hand and we rushed across. Looking back, we were relieved that there appeared to be no owlers on the road yet. Retracing our steps, we skirted around a field and over the bridge, then back to the road the owlers had used earlier. As we paused before crossing the road, my heart was racing from the exercise and excitement. Then, as a low voice spoke from behind us, my heart seemed to fail completely for several seconds.

"Good evening, friend."

We turned and at first could not see who had spoken. Then he stepped out from behind a bush and I gasped to see a Marsh phantom so close. He was a tall, thin man, bearded and with long, straggly hair. The phantom's grin was partially toothless, his face coloured a dark grey. Strangely, his expression was friendly and the fear in me subsided. He believed that we were owlers; we must do nothing to make him believe otherwise.

"Good evening. A fine night for a successful landing." Thomas spoke slowly and with a gruff sound to his voice.

"You carry no cargo?" the phantom remarked.

"I go ahead with a message and take my brother with me. He is learning our ways," Thomas replied and I nodded in agreement.

"Good luck to you both." The man stepped back into the bushes and we continued on our way.

Not daring to stop, we crossed two fields before we could begin to hope there were no more owlers nearby. When I felt I could barely go much further, not at the pace set by Thomas, he led me into the shelter of some willow trees clinging to the bank of a dyke. His eyes scoured the land before we sank down on the grassy slope to rest for a moment.

"We were lucky then," Thomas said, with relief in his voice.

"Your voice... you had him believing we were owlers." I gazed up with admiration.

"Let's hope he's the only one we meet; it's not over yet."

"I know." I was sombre. "You have put yourself in danger for me and I shouldn't have asked it of you."

"I couldn't let you go alone."

"No, I see that. Thank you. This is the end of it."

"I'm glad to hear it."

He stood up suddenly. We could not rest any longer; some of the owlers might be closing in on us. Soon we were almost at the farmyard; it was a relief to be in a more familiar area. Our earlier steps were retraced, around the back of the dairy, across the yard, then towards the church. Thomas took me as far as the main road.

Before we parted, he turned to clasp me and pull me close; his strong arms were wrapped firmly around me. He let go as suddenly as he had grasped me, perhaps worried that I would protest.

Anna's Story
Chapter Eight

Harvest was our last celebration of the summer and early autumn. It marked the end of a time when our lives had become a little easier. A successful yield would give the nourishment that was necessary for us to live in some comfort during the harsh winter months that were to follow.

Now we rose early in the morning with only the merest hint of sunrise in the sky. As December came closer, my working day became shorter as it was not practical to light the shops. Neither were the housewives inclined to venture out after darkness fell. Frequently, the day started with a walk to New Romney while the Marsh mist was still thick in the air. I wore thicker shifts and a woollen cape, but no amount of layers would prevent the chill from seeping through.

Frosty mornings came, and with them the hindrance of hands so stiff it was awkward to tie a lace or fasten a boot. In some ways I found this weather preferable as we could walk into town more swiftly. Icy tracks were firmer underfoot and the exercise soon warmed me.

At home, we benefited from the heat of the forge keeping some of the damp at bay. I knew we were more comfortable than most. For everyone it was a constant battle to keep beds and clothes dry and the home warm. Our diets changed from fresh fruit, vegetables and meats to salted or smoked meat and fish, pickled vegetables and dried fruits. We welcomed the fresh dairy produce from the farm.

As the days became even colder and darker, our free time centred around the warmth of our fires and neighbours saw less of each other. For those who worked from home it was a lonely time. I had plenty of company during my day at work though and walked to the town and home again with Jessica and her father. As the weeks passed from one Sunday to the next, I saw neighbours from our small parish only at the morning or evening church service.

If our homes became clammy and uncomfortable during these months, our local church was more so. There was no fire to bring warmth to it, to dry out cushions or wall hangings. The smell of damp was strong as we stepped into the tiny building. We grew accustomed to the chill and sometimes brought our own cloth or cushion to sit on. If the sun shone through the stained glass windows then we were encouraged to sing with some enthusiasm. It was good to meet up with neighbours and this made up for any discomfort.

When we felt the winter had been with us for long enough, it was Christmas time. We prepared to celebrate and felt light-hearted, thinking of the festivities to come. My father had asked Odigar to find us a Yule log, which he delivered on Christmas Eve with a friendly nod and Christmas greetings. Mother and I pulled it through the house and carefully lifted it on to the fire, where we hoped it would burn for the whole holiday.

That evening, when the sky was black and stars shone with icy brilliance, we all wrapped up as warmly as we could and left the comfort of our fireside for the Christmas Eve church service. Grass and earth were crunchy beneath our feet but that night the fresh air seemed exhilarating. We carried candles and even my father did not complain about the inconvenience of holding a church service so late. He was a religious man and appreciated the meaning of Christmas, but frowned on the frivolous celebrations that most people enjoyed.

The church looked magical with lamps set along the path to lead the way and a radiating glow from the small lancet windows. As we passed through the porch there was the gentle murmur of friends and neighbours talking quietly, then smiles as they turned to greet us. The lights we carried helped to warm us a little and certainly brought a welcoming atmosphere to the church. Dried petals from the long-gone summer roses brought a sweet scent to the air, mixing with, not concealing, the usual smell of damp.

The parson encouraged us to begin the first hymn and I responded, but my thoughts were of the last summer and adventures shared. My eyes met those of Thomas, who sat with his family, and my foolish heart lurched a little. It was unexpected and I looked away. I missed him though, there was no denying it. Three months had passed and we had barely spoken in that time; there had been few opportunities.

At the end of the service we exchanged Christmas greetings, although we would all return to church in the morning. To my secret delight we were invited to spend the afternoon of the day after Christmas with the family at the farm. My mother made arrangements with Mistress Farley. I smiled brightly as we spoke with her and Ellen, hoping in my heart for opportunities to be with Thomas. Then I scolded myself for those silly ideas.

We lingered for just a few minutes before the chill in the air persuaded us that it was time to return to the relative warmth of our homes. Hurrying home, and then to bed, we looked forward to the special day to come.

As dawn broke, I heard Mother in the kitchen. She was preparing the goose for roasting over the fire. I rose from my warm bed, quickly pulling on my woollen shift and thick stockings, then my skirt and bodice. Finally, I tied on my apron as there were plenty of chores to be done before the morning church service. Then we could look forward to our Christmas feast and relaxing in front of the fire.

When the tasks were completed, we were warmed through with a nourishing breakfast of porridge. The table was cleared and the kitchen fire made safe. It was time to leave for church and we waited for my sister, Eliza. She had accepted an invitation to join us for the Christmas Day meal.

"Where *is* Eliza?" Father asked with impatience.

"She'll be doing her best to be ready on time, but what with the children and…" Mother began to defend her daughter.

"There is no excuse to be late," Father interrupted, his dark eyebrows knotted together. "She has healthy children and a good husband; she should be thanking the Lord for her blessings."

We stepped outside, the bright sunshine dazzling us for a few seconds. Father put his hand up to shade his eyes and looked down the track for signs of Eliza and her family. He shook his head with annoyance. We followed him across the road, careful not to slip on the frozen earth.

It was pleasant inside the church that morning; shafts of sunlight lit the dancing dust motes. The air was chilly, but the atmosphere cheerful. Old John was playing his whistle.

It must have been halfway through the service when Eliza made her noisy entrance, interrupting the sermon. She held her baby and was followed by little Bess who clutched the hand of quiet, mild-mannered

William. Not content to sit quietly at the back, she gestured for her husband to follow her along the aisle. The parson waited patiently as she arranged her family, squeezing in beside Mother and asking others to move up to allow space for William and Bess.

Eliza made herself comfortable, brushed stray mousy curls from her face, hitched up her skirt to show a stained shift, then used her sleeve to wipe the dribble from the baby's mouth. Finally she set her dark eyes and snub nose in the direction of the parson, lips in a bored pout.

Father's thick eyebrows were drawn together in the usual frown. Mother, whilst looking a little unsure about the disruption, smiled happily at the sight of her daughter and grandchildren. The parson gave a welcoming nod and the service continued.

When we stepped outside, the fresh air was invigorating; much of the frost had melted and the sky was a vivid blue. My neighbours were in good spirits, pleased to stop and chat for a moment before going home to cook and enjoy one of the best meals they would have in a year.

With Eliza and her family, we returned home. My sister savoured the aroma of the roasting goose and declared that she was looking forward to the feast:

"That does smell good, Mother. My belly will appreciate a good meal! I'll keep Dolly and Bess out from under your feet; William and I can sit on the comfy chairs while you get the meal ready. I know how they can get in the way and we don't want them slowing you." Eliza motioned for William to follow her.

"Dolly?" Father repeated the name in surprise.

Eliza paused and looked at him. "Dolly... Dorothy... the baby."

"Dolly? You spoil those girls' names. Is it not bad enough that you meddle with Elizabeth, who is

80

named after our good Queen?"

"Bess and Dolly, that's good enough for us," Eliza replied cheerfully.

"The meal will be half an hour." Mother tied her apron strings. She accepted Eliza's laziness and Father's bad humour. I doubted that I could be so tolerant.

Mother and I set root vegetables and winter greens over the fire to cook, then cut chunks of fresh bread. Father produced a bottle of wine before opting to sit at the table, rather than be bothered by his grandchildren. The meal was almost ready. I encouraged Mother to join Eliza for a while; she deserved a break. Soon the table was laid, the steaming vegetables set in dishes and the goose in pride of place at the head of the table. Father sharpened the carving knife with vigour and suggested that William fill our cups with fine French wine.

"Now, is everyone comfortable? Do you have all you need?" Mother looked at us all and appeared satisfied, then seated herself. "Eat up, while the food is hot."

"Don't you worry, Mother. This is a rare treat for us, we'll not let it spoil." Eliza took a great spoonful and was raising it to her full lips, meat juices dripping down her dress.

"Not so hasty." Father snapped. "The good Lord must be thanked for this splendid meal, and if that means our food is a little cooler, then so be it."

We bowed our heads while Father expressed our gratitude. When he picked up his spoon, we had our cue to begin. With Bess perched on the bench between her parents and Dolly asleep in a basket, the family was complete.

The meal was relished without incident. It was a pleasure to see young Bess enjoying her food and eating nicely under the critical eye of her grandfather. William thanked Mother and me for preparing the meal, in his quiet unassuming way. Eliza patted her stomach in appreciation and said it was welcome, as she had neither the money nor the time to cook a decent meal like this.

It was the tradition to give presents on New Year's day, but Eliza and her family were to spend the day with William's family. Despite my father's misgivings, my mother was determined to see the children open their gifts on Christmas Day instead. The table was tidied and we settled by the fire to exchange small presents. Some were home-made, such as woollen stockings or a lacy handkerchief. Other gifts had been bought from a pedlar: hair clips, a pretty box, or books. The apothecary sold perfumes, dried petals to scent the home, soaps and creams which were popular as presents.

The most pleasure was found in giving the children their gifts. I had bought a doll for Bess; she dressed her in tiny clothes made by my mother. Dolly clutched the wooden handle of a rattle, made by my father, and shook the metal bells. She lay on a thick new blanket protecting her from the rough rushes on the floor.

"Ta very much, very good of you. I had no time for present buying this year, not with these two to look after, as well as a husband," Eliza said, stuffing a marzipan sweet into her mouth. We expected nothing more from my sister.

Mother and I enjoyed entertaining the children while the others relaxed. They sipped on a fine brandy placed on the doorstep the evening before. Eliza chatted occasionally, interrupting Father who read some passages from the Bible to William. I found a wooden crate for Bess and we made a bed for her doll. Mother sang to Dolly, showed her a string of wooden beads and later held her as she slept.

"Well, I must say that I'm pleased to have a break." Eliza stretched her stout legs out on the hearth. "Our Anna is a natural with the babies, don't you think, Mother?"

"Bess is certainly having fun," agreed Mother.

"You'll be getting wed and having one of your own in no time, Anna. Then you'll know what hard work is, pleasing your husband and caring for the home and babies!" Eliza chuckled to herself. There was a loud tut from my father; this was not a topic to discuss in front of an unmarried woman.

"You enjoying the Christmas story?" Eliza asked William, who nodded happily. "Father reads it well," she continued. "It's nice for William, him not being able to read, and I was never that good at it."

After a while William suggested it was time to walk home before dark. His domineering wife agreed and everyone helped them to gather their belongings. William thanked us for a delicious meal; they wrapped up warmly and were soon gone, leaving just the three of us again. The last we heard of them that day was Eliza calling out to young Bess, telling her not to run in case she slipped.

The following day, it was a treat to have more time free from work and with different routines. I was looking forward to going to the farm; we could be sure of good company and tasty food. It was not long after our midday meal when the three of us set off down the road and along the farm track. I was excited, more than that – there was quite a knot in my stomach. I tried to ignore the feeling of anticipation and told myself that there was no need for it. What was there to get all flustered about?

It was Mistress Farley who answered our rap at the door and ushered us in. We stepped straight into the large kitchen and living area which was full of seasonal scents. There were massive logs smouldering in the fireplace, mouth-watering smells of fresh meat pies and the fragrant aroma of spiced wine, reminding us that it was Christmas time. Faces turned to look at us as we entered, pleasant, smiling faces, and there were murmurs of greeting. Some guests were very familiar and a few I recognised as relatives of the family.

Farmer Farley stood up. "You know my brother, his wife and three daughters from St Mary in the Marsh. We don't have their Andrew with us today; he's needed on the farm. And over there is my second cousin, he's come from Orgarswick so will be staying for the night."

There were smiles and few words exchanged as people made space and welcomed us. The room was crowded: Ellen sat on the floor with her two younger cousins on thick rugs; extra stools and boxes were brought from bedrooms or even the barns. It seemed as if the room was full to its capacity, but someone was missing.

"Thomas has just gone out... won't be a minute he said... just gone to check on Robert. He had a problem with a ewe." Mistress Farley volunteered the information as I looked for the missing face.

"The farmer's lot," commented her husband. "Never a day off."

"We have a good life nevertheless, I can't complain." His wife smiled, offered us a drink of the spiced wine and gestured for us to sit down.

I relaxed in the pleasant atmosphere, a warm drink in my hand and a fairly comfortable box to sit on. Nathan reminded me that I had last met his cousin Lucy at the May Day celebrations in New Romney and said she had recently become betrothed to a butcher, whom she had known most of her life.

We spoke about Lucy's plans, leading me to wonder what my life had in store for me. She was about my age and had her future settled.

I saw my mother sitting down to talk with the two farmers' wives. There were, no doubt, stories to be exchanged: events of interest in our neighbouring village; complaints about the hardships brought by the winter; the latest news from our families – births, deaths, marriages. Not forgetting, and most stimulating of all, gossip and speculation!

The men played shovel-board and draughts. There was some laughter from Farmer Farley and his brother as they tried their skill at guiding a coin on the board. Draughts was a more serious business, which my father preferred.

The door opened and there was Thomas, his eyes bright and cheeks red from the cold air, as he gave a smile to include everyone. He took off his leather boots and thick woollen jerkin, then vigorously rubbed his hands together to warm them. With a few long strides he had picked up a stool in one hand, a plate of marzipan sweets in another and joined Nathan, Lucy and me.

"Good to see you here, Anna. How was your Christmas Day?"

"The children were lovely and we had a good meal." I smiled at him, losing myself for a moment in those brown eyes then looking away quickly in case he should see how pleased I was to see him. "You had problems with a sheep, we heard."

"Silly animal, got herself stuck in a hawthorn hedge and rubbed her skin raw on her hind leg."

"We've been talking to Lucy about her wedding plans," Nathan told Thomas. He looked quite intently at his brother, eyebrows raised. Perhaps he was thinking of a possible announcement about a family wedding.

"I'm looking forward to your wedding when the spring comes." Thomas smiled at his cousin.

"Next it will be Anna – no doubt a pretty girl like her will have to fend off suitable men," Nathan grinned.

"Don't be foolish," Thomas spoke a little sharply. "Show some respect."

We talked a little more, about the family Lucy would be joining in New Romney, the prosperous shop on the High Street and the useful links the marriage made between her own farming family and a local butcher.

"No more work on the farm for Lucy," Nathan commented.

"It will be different, but there'll still be plenty of work to do," Lucy said, smiling back.

I had met her a few times before and liked her a lot; she seemed to be always cheerful and content with her life. Nathan could try to get her to rise to his bait, but would have little success. I would enjoy seeing her when I was in the town and make the time to stop for a talk.

"I'm sure Lucy will be working in the shop, but to have a Sunday off, now that will be a treat," Thomas commented. He looked thoughtful, took a marzipan sweet then commented to no one in particular: "It takes a resilient character to be a farmer's wife. She needs to understand that the farm needs care all hours a day, every day."

Another reference to Abigail, I thought to myself. I was sure Lucy's wedding would not be the only one in the Farley family. The sooner the better, then there would be no excuse for my foolish admiration for Thomas. He was right: Abigail was, no doubt, ideal for the role. Taking a large gulp of my drink, I let the strong taste fill my senses and was determined to put all these thoughts aside and enjoy the day. With a bright smile on my face, I looked towards Nathan. It faltered a little for he was staring right at me, as if he could read my thoughts.

Our little group was broken up as Ellen and her two girl cousins came and suggested that we play some games. We all agreed and, within minutes, had formed a lop-sided circle, more of an oval. Ellen sat in the centre. My father and Farmer Farley's cousin – I forget his name – decided to continue with their draughts. The others joined us for our game. Ellen was blindfolded; she turned herself in circles several times, then pointed to someone. This person had to answer her questions in a strange voice, perhaps squeaky or gruff.

Many giggles followed as people tried to disguise their voices with varying degrees of success. It was often the laughter giving away the identity of the person. Once recognised that person then went to the centre of the group and it started again. It was probably the antics of the blindfolded person that caused the most laughter. As they turned in circles we all flinched, expecting to be trodden upon. Then after turning several times, the person sometimes felt quite giddy and almost fell as they stopped revolving.

The laughter was infectious and we were a noisy group. I felt the disapproving eye of my father upon me, but did not let him spoil my fun. Then Mistress Farley said she had laughed so much that she really must stop for a moment and have a drink. We all agreed.

Ellen suggested we play hide and seek in the yard. Some comments were made about the cold, but it was decided that it would be fun for a while. Our parents preferred to stay in the by the fire and said they would enjoy some peace and quiet. That left Nathan, Thomas, Ellen, their three girl cousins and me; we were soon wrapping up warmly and spilling out into the weak winter sunlight.

We took it in turns and I think that we all preferred to be the one who was seeking as it was warmer to be moving. Those who were hiding made use of the barns, rather than face five minutes or more in the chilly breeze. The sun was becoming lower in the sky and Thomas said the next turn really must be the last. Lucy agreed and said her parents would be calling them any minute to say that it was time to go home.

I decided that a hiding place amid the straw in the barn would be quite warm and comfortable. The door was ajar and I stepped in. It took time for my eyes to adjust to the dim light while I surveyed the area. I found a cosy hide. The straw was rough but smelt pleasant and it was warm as I had hoped. When the barn door opened a little, I was momentarily disappointed, having hoped to remain hidden for some time. Then I saw that the intruder was not Ellen who searched for me but her eldest brother.

"Anna?" There came a coarse whisper.

"Over here."

"Is there room for two?"

"It's not allowed," I replied seriously, but with a slight smile.

"I've missed you." Thomas ignored the rules and made himself comfortable in my snug den.

My heart thudded uncomfortably; surely he could hear it.

"I enjoyed being with you last summer. Not all the worrying though... I don't miss that," Thomas continued. Then looking straight into my eyes: "Tell me you've had your interest in the owlers satisfied."

"I won't go out at night again," I told him, hoping my interest in him was not betrayed by my eyes. "You needn't worry about me; you have more important things to think about."

"More important things?"

"The farm... and..."

"And...?"

"Nathan tells me there could be a marriage between you and Abigail..." I shouldn't have said that; should not have spoken about his private life. Embarrassed, I looked down at the straw and twisted a piece this way and that around my fingers.

Thomas was quiet for a second. Then he said: "Nathan should grow up and stop his teasing; any fool can see that there is only one woman for me to be thinking about... Anna... look at me."

Slowly I untwisted the straw, then lifted my face. Wanting to see that my love for him was returned. Scared that I had misunderstood; that my hopes would be crushed.

"There is only one woman for me," he repeated, and I knew I had taken his meaning correctly.

"Oh..." was all I could say, completely inadequate, but no other words came.

"When I said that it needed a strong character to be a farmer's wife, I did not mean a farmer's daughter. I think a girl who has braved the Marsh phantoms is resilient enough to help run a farm. We've been through a lot together and I know it has brought us closer than would normally be possible. I'd like to think that we have many more shared experiences ahead of us."

"I hope so too; you've been a great friend to me," I said quietly. Brown eyes looked into grey and his steadfast love was clear to see; my heart raced and throat tightened.

"More than a friend?" he asked.

I nodded as he reached out for my hand, moving closer until he was kissing me gently. We paused but he held me closely.

"I love you, Anna. Marry me?"

"Of course I will."

We kissed again, his lips gentle yet firm, hands running through my loose hair and beard rough on my face. We had only a minute or two before the barn door opened once more. I quickly smoothed my hair and hoped that I would not appear too flustered.

We ducked down, wanting nothing more than to be left alone for a little longer, to kiss and whisper words of love. Thomas' hand was firmly in mine as we listened to the muffled sounds of Ellen talking quietly to herself, exploring the possible hiding places within the barn. Her footsteps came closer and she tugged at the bundle of straw which hid us from view. A round freckled face appeared and auburn curls were pushed aside as she peered at us.

"Thomas…oh, and Anna too?" Then indignantly, "You're hiding together!"

"Sorry, it won't happen again," Thomas smiled at his young sister.

"You can both help me find Nathan now. I don't know where he is."

We left the comfort of our hiding place, but took with us the warm feeling of knowing that our love was requited and the yearning for more kisses. Our hands reluctantly parted and all we could share were secret glances while we looked for Nathan. He was soon found and the game was over. Time for the farmers to return to the daily tasks that could not be postponed for the Christmas holiday.

"A pleasant afternoon, many thanks." Father shook hands with Farmer Farley. "God save you all."

"A good evening to you all and a prosperous and healthy New Year," the farmer replied.

"Lovely food. We had a wonderful time, didn't we, Anna?" Mother nudged me.

"Aye, thank you." My eyes met Thomas' and I knew it had been the best day ever.

"Anna, I have your cloak here." Nathan beckoned

me. "I'm glad you enjoyed our little party, it's the company that makes it special you know."

I did know, but he was full of comments like that – what did Nathan know? Then Thomas was there, asking Nathan to look for my mother's shawl.

"I shall be speaking with your father next Sunday," he spoke in a low voice.

My radiant smile told him that I was pleased and as I looked over his shoulder, I saw Nathan watching with an amused expression on his face.

It was New Year's Eve. A rap came on our front door, early in the day, half an hour or so before we were due to leave for the Sunday morning church service. Mother answered the door and returned with Thomas following.

"Thomas would like to speak with your father in private. Would you call him, please?"

"If it's not inconvenient..." Thomas looked a little uncertain.

"Of course not."

I called into the garden and received a grunt which I took to mean that my father was on his way.

"And how are your family?" Mother asked.

"They are well."

"Good, good. Well, Henry won't keep you waiting much longer. We'll collect the eggs, shall we, Anna?"

"I'll get the basket."

My heart beat faster and my stomach twisted nervously. Mother looked at me, eyebrows raised; a visitor was welcome, but what did he want with my father on a Sunday? I busied myself with putting on a cloak and tried to avoid meeting her eyes.

We lingered with the chickens, not sure how long the men needed to talk. When Mother, with hesitation, finally opened the back door it was to find that my father was alone. He was reading the Bible; his usual serious expression gave nothing away.

Eventually the Bible was lowered and carefully closed. "Thomas wished to speak to me about your future, Anna, yours and his."

"Oh, Anna!" Mother looked at me, her face showing hope and excitement.

"He asks for marriage between you," Father continued, taking no notice of the interruption. "The Farley family are respectable and he should provide well for you. As the oldest son, the farm will be his one day."

"This is wonderful news, Anna! You are pleased? I have always found him to be a pleasant young man." Mother was clearly delighted.

Father gave me no time to reply. "Of course she is pleased; it is a good match. He is of fine character. I shall speak to the parson directly after the morning service. I see no reason to delay your betrothal. The contract can take place in a week's time and then we shall be sure that your future is secure."

"If you wish, Father."

"I'll buy some pretty trimmings for your Sunday skirt. I must go to New Romney tomorrow, and the sewing will take no time at all." I could see my mother was already imagining me standing before the parson in a dress lovingly decorated by her.

The matter was settled, as far as Father was concerned. Mother continued to be enthusiastic and chattered about the betrothal, the wedding date and how I would find life at the farm. I smiled back at her and remained quiet, hugging my happiness to myself and savouring the moment.

We were almost late for church, and would have been if Father had not hurried us and frowned upon Mother's chatter. The Farley family looked around and gave smiles as we entered; they obviously knew Father had accepted Thomas' proposal. I sang happily, thanked God for my good fortune and tried to concentrate on the sermon. Inevitably my thoughts strayed when I caught Thomas' eye, and I thought of our future. The service ended and Father immediately sought to speak with the parson in private. Mother and I walked outside into the pale, wintry sunshine and were greeted by Mistress Farley, who was keen to tell us how pleased she was about the betrothal. Thomas and I stood by, allowing our mothers the pleasure of discussing our future. There was no opportunity for us to speak alone.

Father left the church and Farmer Farley separated himself from Isaac in order to speak with him. After a few moments, Thomas joined them and later they came to stand with us.

"I'm pleased to hear you will be joining our family, Anna." Farmer Farley stood tall, his bronzed skin creased with laughter lines. "I knew my son would choose well."

"Thank you. I hope to make him very happy."

"You will, dear, and it will be a pleasure to have another woman in the house." Mistress Farley gave my arm a squeeze and I knew I was lucky to be marrying into this friendly family.

"The betrothal is settled for next week," Father said, giving a rare smile.

"We'll enjoy a fine celebration next summer," Mistress Farley said with enthusiasm, and it seemed that she was picturing the tables laden with good foods and much merrymaking.

"Next summer sounds ideal." Mother nodded with approval.

In the week before the betrothal, the skies were filled with heavy purple-grey clouds warning of snow on the way, then it fell heavily and the land was a gently undulating sheet of white as far as the eye could see. Farmers were busy bringing their flock closer to their farms and telling each other that if the winter was harsh they would be rewarded with thicker fleeces to sell in the summer. But the summer was still far away and for now life was hard.

It took twice as long to walk to work in the mornings and the journey was hazardous. By the evenings, the track was easier if there had been a thaw, but Father and I left Romney at dusk and by the time we reached Hope, the land was in darkness with no light from the moon to guide the way. The snow clouds eventually passed and clear skies brought freezing conditions; the snow became hard and very slippery.

There was no excuse for me to visit the farm. Mother would collect dairy produce during the daytime. It would be foolish to venture out without very good reason between dawn and dusk, or at any other time. I didn't expect Thomas to call on me, and so when the day of our betrothal came, I had not seen him alone since the day he asked me to marry him.

It was bitterly cold, yet I did not notice the chill when the time came for us to stand before the congregation. I stood tall, facing Thomas and said my vows with pride, certain I had a good future ahead of me.

"I, Anna, do willingly promise to marry thee, Thomas, if God will, and I live, whensoever our parents think good and shall meet; till which time, I take thee for my only betrothed husband, and thereto plight thee my troth."

The vows were repeated by Thomas and I could see the love shining from his eyes. How lucky I was that this was no marriage arranged to suit our fathers. The promise was sealed with a gentle kiss, followed by some cheering, and an exchange of gold rings with a simple pattern engraved upon them.

Anna's Story
Chapter Nine

It was a few months later, towards the end of May, when my life was turned upside down. People who I believed I knew, those I had known all my life, turned out not to be as I expected. The worst part of it was not understanding why there was such animosity towards my family. Or was it the moment when I finally grasped the meaning of what had happened, and the consequences it would have for my mother and me?

When I look back, I wonder if I was foolish not to notice the signs that something was about to happen. I had been happily preparing for my life as Thomas' wife and so perhaps was blind to other matters. My father had shown a little interest in my marriage and had even set William the task of making some tools for the farm, as a gift from our family. He told me he was pleased that both of his girls were settled. My mother mentioned to me that Father seemed a little happier and maybe he now accepted his lot. The atmosphere in our home was more relaxed than I remembered it being before.

We had not been up for long that particular morning; Mother was lighting the kitchen fire and I was preparing breakfast. There came a loud rapping at the door. It was so unexpected and we feared bad news; why else would someone call so early? Mother opened the door and Old John stepped in.

"Where is he? Henry?" His gruff voice was raised slightly and his eyes darted around the room.

"I've not seen him this morning, John. He must have left early; he'll be in the forge." My mother looked surprised, but unconcerned.

"Not seen him? Neither of you?" he asked, eyes narrowing with suspicion. We both shook our heads and, seeing the innocence in our faces, he left as abruptly as he came.

"I always said he was a strange man." My mother frowned a little but there were jobs to be done and she continued with them.

We prepared breakfast and when the porridge was heated and thickened, Mother asked me to go to fetch Father from the forge. The door to it was open but the place was silent. The fire had burnt out, tools hung from the walls and the work that was in progress lay waiting completion. The sweet smell of iron hung in the damp air. Clearly Father had not been working there that morning. I returned to the house.

"There's no sign of Father. The fire's not been lit."

"How strange. He must have gone out on other business, although I can't think what."

The front door opened, we both turned towards it. "Good morning, Mother, Anna." William appeared, a little unsure of himself. "Henry's not in the forge. I thought he might..."

"We've not seen him, William. He left early, business in town I expect." Mother patted the bench beside her. "Sit yourself down, there's porridge that will be going to waste if he's gone off somewhere."

"I know nothing of any business." William frowned as he considered the idea. He spooned in some porridge and then recalled: "I saw a man on the way here; I don't know who he was, asking for Henry and said he would be along later."

"It seems as if there's plenty of work for today, that's the second person wanting him this morning." Mother scraped the last of the porridge from her bowl. "Time to get the fire lit, William, or Henry won't be pleased."

It must have not been long after, for I had only fed the hens and tidied the kitchen, when there was another rap on the door. This time it was Odigar, and it was at that moment it struck me what Father was involved in. First Old John and then Odigar were looking for Father and they were the only two who I knew for certain were bound up with the illegal trade. It seemed clear that Father was also embroiled. Later, when I had the opportunity to assess the situation, I realised how foolish I had been. I had been blind to all the signs that could have told me my own father was an owler.

"He's not in the forge; where is he then?" Odigar came straight to the point.

"If it's Henry you want, we've not seen him this morning. He must have risen early," Mother replied calmly. "You'll find William in the forge; he can help you."

"William," he said, lips curling with scorn, "I've no need of him."

"Well, I'm sorry. Can you leave a message?"

"None that's suitable for the ears of two women. He's not been seen today, you say? *If* he does return, there will be some explaining to do and the scene will be none too pretty." Odigar strode over to the window and looked out into the garden, then continued: "I'll be looking out for him. We have unfinished business."

With a last glance around the room, Odigar left us. Mother and I looked at each other in bewilderment. My head was buzzing with all kinds of suspicions and concerns. None of those thoughts could be sorted into any rational order. What had Father done and where *was* he?

Mother sat down suddenly at the table; she was shaking and held her head in her hands. She knew now that something was very wrong.

"Mother... I..."

"Sorry, Anna. I'm being foolish. It's just so unpleasant to have those men in here, looking for your father and so angry with us. I wish I knew where he was."

"We can only wait and see. I'll stay at home today, at least until we have some answers. I can't leave you until he's found."

Mother got up and began frantically sweeping as if to push the worrying thoughts from her mind.

"Mother, we need to talk," I said, taking the brush from her hand.

"Look at this dirt; what will your father say if he comes home to this mess?"

"We need to talk about Father." I sat back down at the table and forced myself to continue, not knowing how to put my words into thoughts. "Have you noticed anything strange, about him, I mean? Did he go out at night?"

Mother turned to me. "Out at night?" she repeated, her voice a little high. "There's not much to tell, Anna. He did on occasion; he was not afraid of the Marsh spirits, or so he told me."

"Why did he go?"

"I don't know. He said that he had things to do... things that would make our lives easier. One day we might even be able to leave this Marsh and live somewhere healthier."

"Do you know what he was doing?"

"He said that it wasn't my concern, but was all for the good of the family. I knew better than to ask questions. Your father is a very private man. He went out in the night and returned two or three hours later, sometimes he went out the next night, too, other times he did not go out for another week, another month, or more. I couldn't complain; he brought us leather, our fine lace shawls and quality wines to enjoy. There was money too; we were not to spend it but keep it until we had enough."

"Enough for what?"

"To lead a more comfortable life," she admitted. "Somewhere else."

"You were to leave all your friends and family?"

"That's what he wanted, but I never believed it... never thought it would happen."

We sat in silence for a moment as I digested the information. Had the time come when he was able to live out his dreams? It was clear Mother deserved to know anything I could tell her.

"There is something I learnt recently. It's about how they, our neighbours and the farmers, earn extra money. And how we have things like good wine and cloth."

I told Mother about the smuggling in and out of the country, of the owlers in their disguises and as much as I knew of the organisation. She listened, asking the occasional question, as I had done when I learnt of the trade.

"Do you think your father was involved?" Her face looked strained, more so than before.

"It seems like he must have been," I admitted. "I'd never thought of it, though, not until today."

"You didn't see him then?"

"I wouldn't have known it was him."

"I can't believe Thomas would let you do it, Anna." She pressed her fingers on her temples, as if to push away the pressure building.

"He didn't... he came to protect me." I reflected on those nights, "I shouldn't have asked it of him."

"This is too much, Anna." Mother stood up, causing the stool to fall over. "I have to do something. I have to keep busy until he returns."

All we could do now was wait until Father came home; at that point we still believed that he would. I was tempted to go to Thomas; surely he may have heard something that could answer some of our questions. But Mother asked me to stay with her; she was feeling nervous after our visitors and it wasn't fair to leave her alone.

We decided that it was best to become involved in some activity, the time would pass faster and some fresh air might clear our heads. We covered ourselves with large, rough aprons and resolved to tackle the weeds in the vegetable plots. They thrived during the spring and we worked hard at raking the ground around onions, peas, cabbage, skirret and carrots. The more the thoughts of Father's connections with smuggling invaded our minds, the more ferociously we tore the weeds from the earth. At last we stood back to survey our work.

"I feel better for that," my mother declared. "We'll probably go back in to find your father at the table with a tankard of ale, or at work in the forge, with no idea of the worry he has caused."

"I do hope you are right," I replied, but with little hope.

There was no sign of Father. Our spirits dwindled again and we wandered around aimlessly, attempting to concentrate on a task, then giving it up in favour of another. We ate some bread and cheese, which we neither wanted nor tasted. It was early afternoon when there was another rap at the door.

"Good afternoon, Farmer Farley." It was a relief to see a friendly face. "Do come in. Mother is here with me."

"Hello, Eve... Anna." He smiled at us, but it was

an empty smile.

"Will you sit down? A glass of ale?" Mother asked, attempting to sound more cheerful than she felt.

"No, I'll not be stopping. I was just wanting to know if you had seen anything of Henry?"

"We've not seen him all day," Mother replied.

"Was there a reason why you wanted to see him?" I ventured to ask.

"Just a matter of some money he owes me, don't worry yourselves about it." Farmer Farley backed towards the door, "Let Henry know that I was asking after him when you see him."

"Money?" I asked.

"A little business between us."

He was gone and we were left looking at each other in bewilderment. Why would Father owe the farmer money? I thought over all that I knew. The farmers left wool-packs to be taken to the beaches and then on to France. The French smugglers would pay for the wool and the farmers and owlers were paid for their wool and their labour. Could it be that my father had been asked to pass on some money to the people in our village and he had not done so? I voiced my opinion to mother. She reluctantly agreed that it seemed likely.

"We need to know if Father has gone, and must see if he has taken any of his belongings with him." I thought it was time to face the truth.

"You are right, Anna. I think we both know, but I did want to cling on to some hope he will return. There might have been an accident and he would not think kindly of us looking through his belongings."

"We have to do it and then we shall know. If he has taken nothing then we will have to start a search."

"Shall we look at his clothes?"

"Aye."

We went to the bedroom and opened up the trunk in which he kept them. They were mainly tunics and breeches of a rough material, suitable for his work in the forge. Nothing appeared to be missing. Mother looked relieved but there was one more place to look. In the cupboard where Mother hung her best dress and Father hung up his Sunday clothes, nothing was hanging from his hook. Mother nodded in acceptance.

Then we went downstairs and looked beside Father's chair, the chair in which he relaxed with his Bible or any political or religious pamphlets he obtained. The Bible was gone and perhaps some of his other reading matter.

"There is no doubt now." Mother sighed heavily and sank down into the chair. "To think that he could do this to us; to plan to leave his family and steal from his neighbours."

"He was a bitter man and had never been happy living here."

"He waited a long time; we should have left when you and Eliza were small. We could have made a new life for ourselves, while we were young enough to do so."

"Perhaps he waited until Eliza and I were settled. Maybe that was his reason for leaving at this time. Maybe he did care?"

"You could be right," Mother reflected. The tears now began their silent descent down her cheeks. "You'll marry Thomas and William can manage the forge. The family can survive without him. Perhaps Eliza and William will come to live here; it will be more convenient for William and it will be lovely to have the children running around. I'm sure Eliza will appreciate the help."

"There, you see things are looking better already."

We stayed at home that afternoon, not wanting to

come across anyone who claimed they were owed money. I wanted to go to see Thomas, but couldn't leave Mother. I'd have to go to the farm the next day; we needed milk and butter. At the end of the afternoon as William left to go home, Mother told him that we would appreciate a visit from Eliza the next day. There was important family business to discuss with her.

It was not until the evening when Thomas came. What a relief to open the door and to see a friendly face. I threw myself towards him and felt all the tension leave my body as his strong arms enveloped my body. My head lay against his chest, his chin rested on the top of my head. I wanted to stay like that forever, not to face any more of that fateful day.

We needed to speak though. "It's been a terrible day," I began. "First Old John and then Odigar were here asking for Father. We didn't know why they would want him... we had no idea, how could we? Then Mother and I spoke and she told me that Father went out at night... he was earning money... she didn't know how. After that it all made sense; he was involved with the smuggling."

"Oh, Anna, how awful for you to find out in this way."

"Did you know?"

"Did I know about your father? No... at least I could not be sure, but I did wonder."

"Your father was here too, my father owed him money and others too. That's what I don't understand: if my father was an owler, why does he owe money? Was he asked to pass it on?"

"It's more than that. People are angry. They have been cheated, both farmers and owlers. There were only a few people who knew who was organising the whole operation on this part of the Marsh and these people will no longer keep the secret, not now that they have been betrayed. They are saying your father was the man who arranged everything; he took the money for the wool and fled. I wish it were not true, but it seems as if it is."

"How can it be? You knew my father, he was a reclusive man."

"He was an intelligent man. He had experience of a world away from the Marsh. Aye, he was an unsociable man, not one to work in a team of owlers, much more likely that he worked alone to organise everything. When you think about it, you'll see that it makes sense."

"I can see, when you say it like that."

"How do you feel about it?"

"I'll have to think about it... and tell Mother... of course, now I must tell Mother. We need to understand what has happened, thank you. But would you mind going home now? I must be with Mother; she needs my support."

"I understand." Thomas stood up and took both my hands in his. "You know that I love you, Anna, and that you have the support of my family... your new family. We must meet tomorrow – will you be able to?"

"We'll be needing milk. I'll come to the farm when I return from work in the afternoon."

We clung to each other for a few minutes before he left. If only he could stay longer; if only we were already married and Thomas could always be there to comfort me. I was being selfish, for in a month we would be together but my mother faced an uncertain future. I watched him walk slowly away down the road, then turned back into the house. It was time to tell my mother the full story.

Mother took the news calmly. I think she was relieved to know all the details. She nodded in acceptance and made no attempt to deny that it could be true. It had been an exhausting day and she could cope with no more; there would be questions to come another day.

I spent a restless night, no doubt worse for Mother than it was for me. I kept going to look out of the window whenever I heard the slightest noise, hoping that Father was returning. It was foolish of me; he would not be back. My father had spent more than twenty years of his life wanting to leave this village and would not return.

Neither Mother nor I were refreshed from the little sleep we'd had. My dreams were confused images of Father as a demon or witch, commanding me not to ask questions, not to go out at night. Then it was Odigar threatening me, for I knew the secrets of the Marsh. The images became confused as I tossed and turned.

When I came downstairs, it was to find Mother at the kitchen table, her head in her hands. She looked up and attempted a smile, but her face was pale and her eyes had dark rings around them. In front of her was a pile of money, not a huge amount, but perhaps more than I would earn in six months.

"I couldn't sleep last night," Mother began and I nodded with understanding. "I was wondering what your father did with all that money that he must have earned when he organised the smuggling. We've been comfortable, but I was thinking that he must have been putting most of it aside, saving up for this time."

"Aye," I agreed. "He was preparing to leave us and then he had an idea that would give him far more money."

"There was a time, perhaps a year ago, I saw him doing something by the fireplace. He was replacing a stone. When I asked what he was doing he told me that he kept some private papers there. It was none of my business and I thought no more of it." Mother picked up some of the coins and let them fall back onto the pile. "I just thought that I would have a look, to see if there was anything of importance. I found this money there; he left it for us."

"He must have a great deal if he could afford to leave us some."

"I imagine he did, but at least he left some for us." Mother sighed.

"I think you should put it back," I told her.

"Why?" Mother asked in surprise.

"We don't know who will be here, looking for money, wanting their payment. Keep it hidden until this is forgotten." I handed her the leather bag of coins.

"You're right." Mother replaced the coins and put them back in their hiding place.

"Now I must hurry if I'm to be on time for work. Try not to worry too much and I'll be home in the afternoon. I'll collect the milk from the farm first."

I had to continue as usual; there were few acceptable excuses for being absent from work. For the first time since my father's departure I left the house. Meeting up with Jessica and her father, we spoke of mundane matters, while all the time I wondered if they knew, if the news had spread to them

I met William, halfway between Hope and New Romney and paused to speak with him briefly.

"Is Eliza able to see Mother today?" I asked.

"Aye, we've had a talk and she'll be along this afternoon. She's wanting to be in town for when the fish comes in and she'll walk along after that."

"Very well, I'll see you later, William."

"Any sign of your father?"

I glanced uneasily towards Mr Browning and Jessica. "No, not yet."

The day was mundane, but I was agitated and made simple mistakes. I worried about Mother and fretted over not knowing if there was news of Father.

On my way home, I spotted Odigar working on the roadside, clearing out some debris from a dyke. I hoped to pass by unnoticed but he looked up and called out to me: "Your father home yet?"

"No," I replied.

He turned away, but it was enough to leave an uncomfortable feeling in the pit of my stomach.

At the farm, I met Ellen working in the dairy. She was turning the handle of the great wooden churn to produce butter. The table was scrubbed clean and the pats were ready to shape the butter when it was ready. There was a pot of dried marigolds; some had been added to the milk to make the butter a golden colour.

"I can't stop," Ellen spoke, without taking a pause from her work. "Take some milk, it's over there."

I filled my jug and left some money.

"Is Thomas nearby?" I asked.

"No, he had to go to check on the boundaries." She gave an apologetic smile.

"It's a busy time of the year." I tried to hide my disappointment.

When I got home I found Eliza there, sitting on a bench, feet resting on the hearth. Bess ran around singing, tugging at her mother's and grandmother's skirts. Her long mousy hair hung all around her face and would have looked better for a good brushing; her clothes were stained and in need of patching. Eliza mainly ignored her, apart from reaching out to deliver a slap when the child bumped into her. The baby, Dolly, was crawling dangerously close to the fireplace. It was my mother who scooped her up and wiped the dribble from her chin.

Eliza had been told about my father; whether by

my mother or some other means I did not know. She was in the process of rejecting the offer of returning to her old home.

"We're settled in our little house; it's nothing special but the leak in the roof has been repaired and the back door shuts properly now. I like to be in the town; the shops are handy and there is always someone to look out for the children. It would be nice to have you there to help out, and who knows when there might be another on the way, but I would rather stay where we are. Maybe you could come and do a bit, now you don't have Father, and Anna will be off soon."

"It's your choice, of course," my mother replied. "I just thought that you might be pleased if I could help with the children, washing and mending clothes, cooking the meals and it would be handy for William."

"Oh, it's no trouble for him to walk here for work; no doubt he'll earn a good living now he's running the forge. Perhaps he can take on a local boy to train up. He could bring in a bit of mending as you have offered; it will keep you occupied in the evenings."

"As I said, it is your choice, Eliza. Shall we take the children out into the garden and we can pick some fresh vegetables for your supper?"

My sister had always been sullen and bad-mannered; more recently she had become lazy towards housework and care of the children. However, her lack of consideration towards our mother astounded me. Could she think of no one but herself? I tidied up the mess made by the children and was glad that Mother was not to become Eliza's cook, cleaner and housemaid.

Eliza and the children went to see William at work in the forge. Mother flitted from one task to the next, frequently looking out of the window. She was nervous to think of Bess and Dolly roaming freely in such a dangerous place. When the whole family had left, she let out a sigh of relief and turned away from the window.

"Was Eliza not upset about Father?" I asked as I started preparing our supper.

"You know what she's like; I expect she was surprised but the children keep her busy and we had little time to talk about it." Mother made excuses for Eliza as I expected her to.

"I'm sorry; you must be disappointed. I know that you were hoping they would move back here."

The full impact of my father's betrayal came to light the following Sunday. We went to church only to find ourselves shunned by the other members of the congregation. Friends and neighbours turned away, ignored our greetings or muttered a reply. It was all the more obvious in a village as small as ours.

Even the Farley family avoided making eye contact with us, leaving me feeling confused and humiliated. Jessica looked rather uncertain and upset; she kept glancing in our direction. Like me, she couldn't understand why the sins of my father were to cause such bitterness towards Mother and me. Thomas looked at us but, to my surprise, made no move to join me.

Mother and I did not linger in the churchyard after the service. We thanked the parson for the service, he nodded politely and we left. It seemed as if all eyes were upon us as we walked down the path.

My mother's spirits were low but she tried to remain positive. "They'll be a wedding to celebrate soon," she reminded me. "People enjoy a good feast and a party; they'll soon forget the trouble your father caused when they've food in their bellies and a cup of wine in their hands. It's fortunate you're to marry Thomas Farley. It will be expected that people show respect towards you."

"You're right. They will." I forced a smile, but doubt weighed heavy in my stomach.

It seemed dreadful at the moment, but people's attitudes would soften. It was true, with the wedding in a few weeks' time, the difficulties would soon improve; they could not ignore the bride. We both tried to feel positive and told each other that all was well. But our worries were never far from our thoughts, as we concentrated sewing the hems on our new dresses to be worn for the celebration.

On a Sunday, we would usually attend both church services, but decided to avoid the evening one. Thomas decided to miss it, too; he came to see me instead. I believed his affection and loyalty had never wavered. But, from the moment I opened the door and saw him standing there, I knew something was about to go horribly wrong. He just stood. My tall, strong, hard-working farmer, looking guilty and apologetic. Like a small, lost boy.

"Come in," I struggled to whisper the words. My heart was tight and I could say no more. I waited for his words.

"We need to talk. I'm sorry, Anna." He spoke slowly, reluctantly.

"What is it?" I asked, my throat restricted and limbs heavy.

"People are talking; they are saying that you and your mother will have benefited from your father's secret business over the years. They are wondering if your mother will be going to join your father once we are married."

"You know that's not true."

"The owlers have said that they will no longer sell wool from our farm if we marry. We rely on that money; wool doesn't fetch a high price in the English markets. My father is a proud man: we have farmed the land for generations and we need the support and goodwill of our labourers and the local people."

"There is that much hatred towards our family? It will be forgotten in a few weeks or months surely... after the wedding."

"Father will not take that chance. He says if we marry then Nathan will inherit the farm; he must secure its future."

"*No*." I was stunned, numb inside. "What will happen to us?"

"I have no choice. You know I love you and there will never be another for me. You also know Nathan; he has no love of the land and will neglect the farm. I can't let that happen... I wish... I wish I could. I am asked to choose between you and the land I am meant to farm. I have to make a decision – the hardest decision of my life – but we can't marry. I must put the farm and family first, before my own needs and love."

His hands reached out to mine and we stood in silence. Time stood still, knowing these were our last moments together. Stunned beyond words, I felt unable to respond.

"Never marry?" I finally asked.

"Maybe in a year or more, things change." He smiled slightly.

"I see." I let my hands drop. "I cannot wait for a year or more, perhaps forever, while neighbours ignore me and gossip behind my back. Is it best that we say that we shall never marry, rather than live in false hope?"

"I would rather have hope." He looked distraught, but it was he who had made the decision; it was his doing.

"Goodbye, Thomas." I turned away from him.

"I love you, Anna." Those were the last words I heard from him for a very long time.

I closed the door behind him, then turned away and went to find my mother. There was not much to say and I told her without tears or anger. My emotions were frozen. It felt as if I was talking about somebody else's life.

Mother wanted to hold me, to comfort me. She cried a little about the injustice of it all and begged me to believe Father would never have left, had he known that my future was not secure. Pacing up and down, she fretted about what our life would be. I sat stiffly on the bench, numb and disbelieving.

I can remember little about the days that followed, only that I went through the motions of my usual life. If I saw people from Hope, they averted their eyes, embarrassed by my presence. I walked to and from the village alone and usually saw Jessica during my lunch break, not wanting to cause her difficulties by meeting at other times. She remained a true friend, shocked and upset by my sudden change in fortune. I bought our dairy produce from the town, paying the extra in order to avoid the Farley family.

It was towards the end of that week when Mother had news of how this was affecting her own work. "Annabel had the baby two days ago."

"Oh, why did you not say before? What did she have? Is all well?" I struggled to show some interest.

"I did not hear until today, I think it was a boy; they called for another midwife."

"Oh, Mother... I'm sorry."

There was little more to say, words were not needed to express the significance this had on our lives. Mother had been a respected and much-loved midwife. Her income was needed in order to run our home.

"I did not want to say before, until I had been." Mother stood with her hands outstretched towards the heat from the fire. "I rode to Appledore today, to see my sister. We need to get away from here; there is nothing left for either of us. Emm has a tavern, as you know. It's in the heart of the village and gets a fair amount of trade. She could do with some help since her husband passed away last winter. We can go to live there – what do you think?"

"Go to help Aunt Emm in Appledore?" I frowned, trying to picture us there, not knowing any different from the life I lived between New Romney and Hope. "I don't know... do you think it for the best?"

"I do. We have a little money; perhaps we can rent a small cottage? If your father ever comes looking for us, he will know where to find us. People will not judge us and we can make new friends."

"A new start? Away from this hurt."

Time would heal some of my wounds, people would gradually become more forgiving as their memories faded and they would include us in village life again. However the hurt would still be with us and I would not be Thomas' wife. We had the chance to move away from the miserable memories.

Tomorrow was Midsummer's Eve, usually one of the favourite days of the year for me. It was my birthday, and traditionally we had the Midsummer's Eve party to look forward to. This year, the following Sunday was to have been my wedding day. I knew that I didn't want to spend it in the village.

"You're right," I replied at last. "There is nothing to keep us here; let's go before the weekend. Can we do that? Can we leave before Sunday?"

"I'd do anything to ease the pain that you are feeling and if we can leave before Sunday it will make the day easier for you. We'll leave on Saturday." As Mother made her promise, I felt some relief from my grief and she too smiled a little, now that it was settled.

I didn't go back to work at the apothecary's shop again. Instead, I asked to be released immediately and they let me go.

On the evening of my birthday, Jessica's parents allowed her to spend an hour with me. We talked about our childhood, laughed a little over incidents from the past and spoke of plans and dreams we had shared when we were innocent children. Most of all, we regretted the distance that would now be between us.

"This is the first time I'm allowed to stay the whole evening for the Midsummer party," Jessica reflected. "It doesn't seem so important now you can't be there, and the mystery of Odigar's tales has been solved. Did the Farleys not invite you?"

"I can't be with Thomas, not yet. Not ever."

"It will never be the same without you." She looked into the fire, eyes bright with tears.

"I'll write to you and give the letter to Eliza. Perhaps you'll be able to visit; it's not too far if you journey by horse."

"Thomas will see the mistake he has made; you'll be back in no time and everything will be as we planned." Jessica spoke as if she truly believed her words. "It's just a case of waiting."

"Maybe, but I doubt it will ever be the same." Once I had gone, there would be no going back for Thomas and me. I was certain of it.

Jessica had to leave. With tears streaming down her face, she hugged me. My heart was so heavy it felt as if the depression would never lift.

We were to leave at first light. Our bags were packed with our clothes, bedding and personal possessions. The larder was empty; Eliza had taken the food. The fire in the kitchen was barely glowing; it just needed sweeping out. We would do without hot water or warm food in the morning. William had fixed boards over the windows, to protect them from the weather. It was no longer my home, just a house, empty and abandoned.

I left Mother sadly surveying the cottage where she had spent all her married life. She said she preferred to be alone for a while and would go to bed shortly. For the last time I went to sleep in the room I had once shared with Eliza. It was at that moment I really accepted the changes in my life. Thomas was not going to come back to tell me it had been a terrible mistake, that he would put me before his land and his family, or that the Farleys had relented and would allow us to marry.

Never again would he admonish my recklessness in discovering the secrets of the Marsh, yet be there to help me out of trouble. I would never be held closely, enveloped by his broad body and strong arms, while he whispered his love for me or we kissed with passion.

For the first time since Thomas told me, I cried. Once I started I couldn't stop, the numbness left and my heart was filled with pain. Images filled my mind, from him tenderly ensuring I was comfortable and not scared by Odigar's tales, to the time I was roughly pulled into a hiding place to protect me from the owlers. Then there was the growing friendship, as he trusted me with all he knew of the local smuggling and his suggestions we would always be together. Each memory was more painful than the last and it was all the more poignant that it was exactly a year ago, when our friendship had grown as I trusted him to answer my questions about the ways of the Marsh. By morning my eyes were swollen and red.

There was a light, early morning mist over the land when we brought Bonnie and her cart to the front of the house. Our possessions were soon loaded and, without speaking, Mother shut the front door behind us. We settled in the cart and commanded Bonnie to walk on. Turning back we could just make out the shadowy form of the church and the cottages as we silently said our farewells to Hope.

Jessica's Story
Chapter One

It has been a week, no eight days, since Anna left. A week since she should have married and today I sat in the church again, looking at the slumped figure of Thomas. I know he regrets his decision, of course he does. Theirs was a love match; they were well suited and if her father had foreseen what would happen, surely he wouldn't have left the family at that time. If only he, Mr Smith I mean, had waited another month, Anna and Thomas would have been married and, if her father had chosen to leave at that time, Anna's future would have been secure.

There I was, sitting in All Saints, moving my lips and muttering the responses. But my thoughts were only of Thomas and how wretched he must be feeling, to be there without his bride. I just wish he would go to her, go to Appledore and bring her home. If it was Nathan, he wouldn't think twice about it. But Thomas is more serious and the responsibilities of the farm weigh heavy on his shoulders. I shouldn't compare the brothers and if I were to, even now Thomas must still stand as the better brother. Nathan is careless and work-shy, and I find him quite irritating, but Thomas' sense of commitment to farm and family has caused him to lose his betrothed and me to lose my dear friend.

I am upset and so I ramble in this disorderly way, as I think of Mr Smith and how he cheated his neighbours, leaving his family to cope with the aftermath. And so, they are gone, all three of them. And we, the ones left, remain both shocked at the deceit and mourning their leaving.

But, this isn't what Anna wished me to do with her notebooks. She asked that I continue with my own story, to write of my life here in the tiny settlement called Hope. What do I have to write that could be of any interest? The days continue one after another and the only changes are those of the seasons and the effects they have on our daily routines. For now, Anna's story is my story, it being the only thing I can think of and the most significant event in our parish for many years. I will put her notebooks aside until I have my own tale to tell.

*

I have found Anna's notebooks in the wooden chest in my bedroom. I admit to feeling a little guilty, having left it so long before I continued our diary. I was upset when she left and just put them away, thinking there would be nothing to tell. I was wrong for now I have my own story, which started in the spring of this year 1587. It was a time where there was promise of great changes to my life and it seemed that my future was mapped out before me. It was a significant period as I changed from girl to woman. But plans can change in an instant and once again I found myself unsure of what direction my life would take.

Now a new person has come into my life and I feel an excitement fluttering within me. A new life, a new beginning. I am on the brink of great things, having never imagined my life would amount to anything out of the ordinary. There is the urge to write my story, to continue the tale of the young women who have lived in this small settlement named Hope.

But, I am jumping ahead, without recording the details. I have picked up Anna's notebooks and have resolved to write of my life. I'll go back in time, to start my story in March 1588 and will enjoy the process of sharing my thoughts in these pages.

*

"Jessica, take a break from your chores; come and sit with me by the fire." Father rose from the supper table and gestured to the bench seat. He turned towards my younger brother. "James, go and make sure the chickens are safe for the night."

Sitting on the edge of the wide plank, smooth and glossy from years of use, I gathered a shawl around my shoulders. I looked around the room, focusing on the small details: the shapes caused by the shadowed ridges in the rough, lime-washed walls, and the crushed, split stems of the reeds in the matting on the floor. It was something I had always done as a child: found the features of animal and human faces hidden in the depths of natural materials. Now I resorted to this secret world, rather than face the words Father needed to share.

The reed matting covered a bare earth floor and the uneven walls were decorated with several tapestry pictures. There were two windows, both small and misshapen, one to the front and the other to the back of the cottage. Underneath the window that looked to the front, there was a table with some material on it and a basket beneath containing more fabric. This was where my mother worked. The centre of the room was dominated with our old oak table and benches, where the remains of supper were still scattered. A large cupboard with some shelves above lined the back wall; inside was much of our food, along with cooking and eating implements. There were doors either side of the fireplace, one leading to the small square of a front entrance hall and the other to a staircase..

"Shouldn't I just...?" I looked towards the supper table.

"It can be left for a moment and your mother has gone to draw water from the well; it will be done soon enough. I need to have a talk with you." Father prodded the fire with a length of iron and added another log.

My mending basket was on the side-table and I reached towards it. I was in the habit of keeping busy. There was always something that needed doing and I felt it was my responsibility to help my mother whenever possible.

"Jess, you are such a help to us all and a great comfort to your mother, but please leave your darning for the moment."

"Is it Mother?" I asked. "Tell me she isn't ill." Why else should he need to speak to me, away from James who was still young? When had Father ever spoken privately with me about any matter? Of course there had been times of grief and upheaval in our lives: the death of my young brothers and the revelation that Henry Smith had cheated the owlers. But he had never asked to speak to me alone. "I shall do all I can to ease her burdens... is it the ague?"

"Jessica, your mother is weary as you know, but she has her good and bad days and the bad days are no worse. It is not her health I want to talk to you about." Father stood and placed his hand on my shoulder; it lay there in a clumsy manner, for he was not one to demonstrate his affection. "You have shown yourself to be a reliable and helpful daughter. Your mother and I could wish for no more from you."

"Thank you, Father; I do my best to be useful," I replied. My fingers folded little pleats in the material of my skirt. They were unused to being idle and it gave me something to concentrate on as the fear of what I was about to be told grew and my throat tightened.

"You have some education, enough to be of use to you; any more was unnecessary. It is a girl's mother who can provide her with the most useful skills in life. Cooking a decent meal, housekeeping and needlework; all these things you have learnt from your mother who is a good woman and a fine wife to me.

"Much as we value your help here, it would be wrong to ignore the fact that you have grown into a young woman and would make a worthy wife for any man. I have thought carefully about your future happiness." Father paused for a moment, his chin rested on his hand and he gazed directly into my face for a moment.

"Thank you." I waited for what he had to say, my throat still tight and a feeling of heat rising up through my neck. My fingers no longer pleated folds in my skirt; I was frozen. The bench beneath me felt hard, but I didn't like to move. I couldn't move, as I waited to hear the plans for my future.

"I have been friends with Mr Blackstock of the grocery store in the town for many years. He has a son who you will know of, as you are in New Romney most days. His name is Edmund. He is a good man who can offer a decent home and security for a wife. Jessica... Jess, he would like it if you would be his bride."

"Edmund Blackstock." As I repeated his name, the heat rose to my face. I hadn't thought... how foolish of me not to have thought... about this moment. When Anna was to marry Thomas we had wondered what the future held for me, but that was to be *in* the future. Not any more – it was happening now. It was happening now and how was I to respond? How was I meant to feel?

Edmund Blackstock. I knew him as the person who sometimes served me in his shop. He appeared to be kindly and indeed respectable. We occasionally passed a few words about the weather or he would ask after my family. How strange to think of that person, someone known to me but only as much as I knew any one of the shop-keepers in the town, to think of him and know he was to be my husband. I was neither pleased nor displeased. Perhaps faintly disappointed? I pushed the notion from my mind; squashed the seeds of regret before they took root. There could be no fault in my father's choice of husband for me.

"Father, this is quite a surprise," I began. The heat began to subside from my face and the tension lessened. "I am honoured."

"Are you pleased, Jess?"

"He seems to be a good man. I barely know him, but I trust your judgement, Father."

"It is a relief for me to know that you are to be settled within a good family."

It was all agreed. It had been decided before I even knew of it. A daughter would rarely question her father's choice. There must be questions to be asked, things I needed to know. But my mind was numb and so I learnt no more of Edmund Blackstock and his plans for me.

"Father, would you mind if I could have a little time to get used to the idea before you tell James? I'm pleased of course, but perhaps in a day or two?"

"There is no need for James to be told of your plans yet," Father agreed. "However, we are to meet with Edmund and his family this coming Sunday. We are attending the church service in New Romney and are invited to join them for a cup of wine afterwards. It will give us the opportunity to meet the family in their own home and for you and Edmund to get to know one another."

"It's all arranged then. Thank you, Father." I rose from the bench, and looked back, asking for his permission to leave.

"I am sure your mother will be able to advise you, if needed." Father looked relaxed as he smiled at me, no doubt glad his part of the arrangements was done.

I returned to the normality of the kitchen. Mother gave me a searching look and I attempted a smile in return. She must have been reassured by the slight upturn of my mouth, for she turned back to the heavy pan she was cleaning. My throat was still tight and my stomach knotted as the words from the recent conversation spun around in my head. I needed to keep busy and gathered the candles as dusk was nearing.

No amount of housework could silence those unanswered questions. I tried to imagine what marriage would be like. How could I think of it when I barely knew the man I was to marry? Perhaps it would be easier after Sunday; maybe I would learn the answers to some of my questions. Where would we live? Would he be an agreeable husband? Would his family welcome me? When would we marry?

It was inevitable that I would worry about seeing Edmund Blackstock in the few days before the arranged meeting on Sunday. Dreading an awkward moment, I just hoped he could be avoided. I scurried through the streets of New Romney, my head turned away from the direction of the grocery store, as I went to and from my work at the draper's. My head went light and heart pounded at every movement of the shop door. What would I say... how should I react, if his mother or one of his sisters came into the shop? And if it were Edmund himself in the street, I feared I would just sink to the ground with the fear of not knowing how to respond to him.

It was the very next afternoon, when I had only just heard about my future husband, that I happened to meet him. I was walking to the beach with Ellen, Thomas' sister, and she was chattering away about something, but my mind wasn't really focused. I liked Ellen very much; she became the companion who in some ways replaced my dear friend Anna. Although younger than me, she had a confidence and natural gaiety that I envied. Whenever she had tasks to do in New Romney, my friend would ensure that she sought me out for company on the walk to or from the town, or spend my lunch-break with me.

I think Ellen must have been talking about Bertie, a boy who had just started work at the forge; she was obviously very taken with his friendly character, blond hair and blue eyes. What a change for William, she said. How nice to have someone to work with, rather than be alone all day. I didn't really need to listen to her and found that an agreeable nod was enough to satisfy; her mind was full of this young man. I envied her new romance and the thrill it gave her; all I felt was dread in the pit of my stomach when I thought of my own betrothal.

"I'm sure he's a hard worker; he did such a good job on a tool for Thomas..." Ellen was still speaking about Bertie. But my mind had frozen; I couldn't make sense of her words or respond in anyway.

There he was, walking along the track that led from the beach, striding towards us. How was I going to take another step towards him? I must turn... go back to the town... I had forgotten there was another job to be done.

"Ellen, I need to go to the apothecary first, I need to...."

She wasn't listening and carried on walking.

There was something about Ivychurch; did I know Bertie's family came from the village?

So we approached the shallow beach where the fishing boats pulled in – there was no avoiding him, no other route to take. Edmund was almost upon us, his head held high and a broad smile across his face, which looked a little flushed. I found myself examining his features: mid-brown hair was brushed neatly, his beard was well trimmed, hazel eyes were creased at the sides and his nose was straight. My throat tightened and mouth became dry as I hoped that he wouldn't try to engage me in any conversation. Surely he would pass by with just a friendly nod; that would be enough until our families met.

"Lovely day, Miss Jessica, Miss Ellen." Edmund spoke loudly and with confidence. His smile was broad and he looked well satisfied with his life as he paused before us. I noted that he was not a tall man; I was only a couple of inches shorter.

I still just nodded and smiled. I should have said something. Some form of polite greeting; I couldn't form the words. Edmund did not appear to notice.

"Are you going to buy some fresh fish?" he asked. His words were directed at me, but still I said nothing. "You'll know how to look after me; I like a bit of fresh fish!"

I made some attempt at a reply but the words stuck. It didn't seem to matter and Edmund was undeterred. "You'll have a fine time in our splendid church on Sunday." He nodded in the direction of St Nicholas, with its sturdy tower and fine Norman architecture. "And back to our humble home afterwards." This was accompanied by a self-satisfied smile as he paused for me to object, for his home was not that of a poor man. "Mother and the sisters will make a fine fuss over you; it's all they can talk about."

I hadn't noticed before, when I had seen him in the shop, that his voice was so loud. How he roared his greeting and expressed every word with such relish. Then he was telling me how nice it was to have seen me and with a cheery farewell he was gone. How foolish I felt. Ellen stood there looking surprised while all I could feel was my burning cheeks and the dryness in my throat.

"Father has arranged for us to marry. He told me just yesterday." I had hoped my parents would be the ones to tell friends and neighbours so that I could avoid any awkward questions.

"I didn't realise that you knew him. Isn't he from the grocery? What's his name?" Ellen asked.

"Edmund... it is... Edmund."

"Aye, I recall it now. Are you happy, Jess? What changes you have before you!"

"Happy? I... Aye, I mean, aye of course I am." I said the words that needed to be expressed.

"But, you'll have time to get to know him? Before the wedding, I mean."

"I hadn't thought... we are to meet on Sunday... so I...." A quick meeting after church, a talk in the shop, what else... how would we get to know each other? "No doubt we'll see each other often enough," I said, as I forced a smile.

"And do you think him handsome? He seems decent enough." I suspected Ellen's thoughts were still full of the young worker at the forge. Perhaps she compared the two men.

"Handsome? I hadn't considered... So long as he is kind and respectable, that is all I look for."

I could not fault his appearance, neither did I admire him in any way. What a foolish thought, my father had chosen a decent man and I had only to think of Anna to know there was no point in feeling romantic over anyone. Ellen was still young and caught up with silly notions. There was no more to say and thankfully she did not pursue the subject. I didn't feel able to discuss my feelings, although she may have been sympathetic. My loyalty to my father and the match he had made was unwavering.

A coarse cackle rang out in the sky above me; it was a gull circling on the wind, waiting for the opportunity to swoop on its fish dinner. It screeched out again, mocking me, mocking my foolish ways.

Jessica's Story
Chapter Two

The whole family walked to New Romney on that Sunday morning, at the end of March. As we passed roadside cottages and neared the greens, the thickset tower of St Nicholas Church loomed before me. My limbs felt stiff; how I longed to turn and retreat to our own dear little church. We passed the old priory and walked straight across the High Street, and now the whole of the parish church was in view. There they were, waiting at the doorway: the Blackstock family.

I felt compelled to stare at them, but could not smile or even nod a greeting. He had three younger sisters. They stood together, like three peas in a pod, each one as quiet and serious as the next. Soon there would be four of us, four sisters, all quiet and serious. Would we share confidences and would I, the new sister to them and wife of their brother, be made welcome in their home? Their mother stood over them, checking each one was standing up straight and that their clothes were tidy. She wouldn't fuss over me; I would be a married woman. Or would she?

Edmund and his father moved away from the group. Hands outstretched they strode over to meet us.

"Good morning, pleased that you could all come. It's a fine day to celebrate the joining of our families."

Mr Blackstock greeted us with great enthusiasm.

"Good morning, it is indeed a fine day, a fine day," Edmund echoed his father's words.

"How kind of you to invite us." My mother smiled at everyone.

"Jessica, you know my mother and sisters of course." Edmund placed his hand on my arm and guided me towards them. My body felt as if it were made of wood. I looked back at Mother, she was following. I was deposited before the women of his family and Edmund turned back towards my father.

"What a pretty pendant you are wearing, Jessica." Mrs Blackstock gave me a friendly smile.

"Thank you..." I should have said more, perhaps told her it was a present from my mother.

"Just enough ornament for a young woman, and I always feel that a mid-brown is a most suitable choice of material for a dress."

"I made it myself, with some help from my mother."

"Of course, what useful skills you have to pass on to your daughter, Kate." Mrs Blackstock reached out to to pat my arm

"I hope so. Jessica enjoys sewing don't you, Jess?"

"Aye."

"...And a pleasant change for us to be joining you all here today," I heard my father say. "I can't walk into this church without thinking of that storm and what it must have been like for our forefathers all those years ago. To think those iron rings on the church wall once had fishing boats tied to them, and now the beach is five minutes walk away."

"Our town would have been very different indeed, if it were not for the great storm," Mr Blackstock added. "Imagine the River Rother, here in New

Romney and flowing past your own small village. It would have been very different for us all."

"It would have been very different," my father agreed. "But Romney survived without its estuary, a smaller and humbler place."

"And your own village, even humbler still," Mr Blackstock pointed out.

The men led the way and we women and girls trailed behind with James, who didn't quite fit into either group. I looked at Edmund's back, trying to raise a flutter of interest in him. There was nothing. Perhaps if he had looked back and tried to catch my eye it would have been different.

Mrs Blackstock was still speaking about sewing; I tried to concentrate on her words. "I'm sure your mother has taught you many useful skills, as I do my own daughters."

"Jessica has been a great help to me and I am proud to say that she will make a fine wife," my mother said, and I felt the flush of embarrassment rise.

"There is no doubt of that; we are blessed with only one son and want the best for him," Mrs Blackstock replied.

The three sisters stood just behind their mother, saying nothing but listening with interest. Their eyes were wide and mouths slightly open; how curious they must be about me. We hadn't been introduced. The eldest was perhaps just a year or two younger than me; I wondered what her name was. She knew mine; they all knew my name and in turn I knew nothing about them.

Mrs Blackstock turned to them. "It will be new dresses for you all when your brother marries! We'll be regular customers, choosing our material from the draper's."

"It will be lovely to see you there," I managed to reply.

"And later, you'll work alongside your husband in our shop. It will keep you busy until you have other commitments."

I was spared any more, as she was then absorbed with ushering her three daughters into a pew and beckoned for me to join them. Mother sat beside me, with James joining my father in the seats behind. Turning slightly, I found Edmund looking at me. A blush began to rise and I attempted a smile. He gave a slight nod and smile in return. The service began and, although I tried my very best to concentrate, my thoughts wandered to the future and the time when this would be my place of worship and these strangers around me would be my family.

Once back out in the sunshine, the service was praised. "He does a good reading, our vicar; I'm sure you agree, Jessica." Edmund spoke to me directly for the first time. "And a good choice of hymns I thought... a very good choice."

"It was all very... very pleasant." I looked up at him and began to feel more comfortable. There was nothing to find fault with in either his looks or manner.

"I'm glad you agree."

"A welcome change from your little chapel, no doubt," commented Mr Blackstock

"All Saints suits us well enough, and our small community still manages to enjoy the service," my father responded.

"I hear the roof is in disrepair," Edmund said. He turned to me, "You'll not suffer such discomfort for much longer, St Nicholas is a fine church; no cause for complaint here."

I looked up at the solid building with its long nave

and Norman features. It was a good church, but my heart was back at home with All Saints. I loved our own slim tower and spire, the row of high lancet windows and the ancient carvings around the doorway. But best of all, it was the small mound the church sat upon, which caught my imagination as I crossed the plank bridge over the ditch and wondered about all the people who had walked the path in the centuries before me.

"It's no discomfort," I replied. Edmund didn't hear.

We walked, the two families, away from St Nicholas and to the High Street, then turned towards the Blackstocks' shop, which was a substantial building, with a wide frontage on to the road. The entrance was familiar, but today the shutters were closed and we filed into a dimly lit space, with the storage barrels, shelves and boxes forming indistinct shapes in the gloom. The smell was comforting, that of grains and oils and wood.

No longer a customer, I followed through a doorway and into the Blackstocks' home. A long room, running along the back of the shop, with a substantial fireplace to one end, a large table with benches, and armchairs strewn with cushions and blankets, was obviously the centre of family life. It was furnished in a plain style with heavy furniture of good quality; on the walls tapestries depicted scenes illustrating good Christian morals. Edmund's three sisters immediately busied themselves offering plates of pastries and biscuits, under the ever watchful eye of their mother.

Mother gave me searching looks every now and then and, in return, I smiled my reassurance that all was well. I was beginning to feel more relaxed, even interested to see the place that was to be my new home. I was curious to know what other rooms were upstairs, but I couldn't even see the staircase, it would be enclosed behind the doorway beside the fireplace.

"You'll be married at St Nicholas of course," Mr Blackstock stated as he handed me some wine.

"Oh, I...?" I looked towards my father for guidance.

"Indeed we will; Jessica was impressed with our service this morning. I can see that she will agree it is ideal." My future husband spoke for me.

"It isn't the usual way... our parson, he would expect...?" What would he think of us, if I chose to marry in another parish. Again my throat tightened.

"I like a woman who knows just how things should be done." Mr Blackstock smiled warmly at me. "She has just the right amount of sense, for she sees how it should be but also how it must be."

"There will be no offence, my dear," Edmund patted my arm clumsily. "It is clear that there is barely the space for our families at All Saints, and I can't say that I could let my own mother sit in a puddle if it were to rain. Oh no, she could not be sitting in a puddle on her son's wedding day!"

"St Nicholas is certainly more comfortable and it is no distance for our friends to come." My father had little choice but to concur.

"Well, as we are all in agreement, I see no need to wait. I suggest that I speak to the vicar about a betrothal in the very near future." Mr Blackstock turned to his eldest daughter: "Some more wine for our guests please, Ann."

The very next week, just ten days after my father told me of his plans for my future, I found myself back at St Nicholas church. I recall Edmund's words as we approached and how I blushed to hear them: "Ah, here she is, as pretty as I remembered, here she is."

He was all smiles, looking over me as if I were an animal to be selected at market.

As the heat rose in my neck and face, I looked down at my feet. When I dared to look up again, I saw my future mother-in-law coming towards me, her face all smiles. She took my arm and led the way into the church, Edmund's three sisters following closely behind. It was if I was engulfed by the Blackstock women, with Mother left to walk behind. Uncle Clement followed, the voice of Edmund Blackstock dominating their conversation.

At the end of the service the Reverend announced our betrothal ceremony. While Edmund strode to the front of the church, I had to squeeze past his mother and sisters, apologising for pressing against them and tripping over their feet. Then came the walk along the nave to the chancel, my legs leaden all the way. There I was, standing with Edmund before the congregation, glancing back but not seeing any of them.

When the time came, I didn't know how the vows could be forced out, my throat felt so constricted. However, I stood tall, determined to look into his eyes as I took them and somehow the words came: "I, Jessica, do willingly promise to marry thee...Edmund, if God will, and I live, whensoever our parents think good and shall meet; till which time, I take thee for my only betrothed husband, and... and thereto plight thee my troth."

As I spoke I thought of my good friend Anna and how in love she was with Thomas when they said their vows. How happy she had been that day; I wished I could feel just a little of the way that she had felt. My father had made a good decision though and I respected his choice of husband for me. How foolish to think of Anna and Thomas when their happiness was so short-lived.

When Edmund took his vows, he looked towards the congregation, then back to me. His voice was strong, the words clear: "I, Edmund do willingly promise to marry thee, Jessica, if God will, and I live, whensoever our parents think good and shall meet; till which time, I take thee for my only betrothed wife, and therefore plight thee my troth."

The commitment had been made to one another and plain rings exchanged. Before I realised what was happening, Edmund bent down and placed a brief kiss on my lips. He took my arm in a proprietorial way and led me back to our families.

I felt the pressure of his lips on mine for the whole walk home. As we left New Romney behind us, I stamped my boots on the soft mud of the track and wrapped my cloak tight around my body. The north-easterly wind brought with it a bitter chill, but the promise of summer months was before us. The track was lined with hawthorn trees: spiky, gnarled specimens of no great elegance, but in the spring they were made beautiful by thousands of tiny white flower-heads, and in the winter their red berries glowed among dying foliage and fading colours. I preferred the willow trees that bent with the wind and had long pendant leaves drifting in fronds.

But I am avoiding speaking of my feelings, so I think of the trees and the track that was still muddy from the recent rainfall. I had no feelings to tell of. I was neither happy nor unhappy. My future was nothing to look forward to, nor was I fearful. I could imagine no more than working alongside my husband in the shop, helping in the home and being one of the young women in the household. Yet I would not be one of them, for the sisters were young and unmarried. I would be the new wife, not Mrs Blackstock head of the home. No, I would be the young wife, finding her place among all those women.

Walking home with my parents and James, I tried to think no further ahead than the next few weeks. It was best not even to consider what married life would bring. But, however much I tried to concentrate on the trees and the lambs, my lips were rigid and all my thoughts were on the afternoon walk that had been arranged, and would he... would he dare to press his lips upon mine when we were alone? As his betrothed, was it expected of me to offer my lips to his? If only Anna had been here, I could have asked her advice. But I had no one; I certainly didn't want to concern my mother with my foolish thoughts.

As we approached our cottage, I saw Father surveying the roof. Our own home was in the centre of a row of three cottages made of wood and mud. Topped with thatch, our roof had fresh bundles of the marsh reeds secured into place, neatly pressed in around the small windows. Our bedrooms in the roof space were warm and dry, with the heat from the fire rising through the plank floor and the wind and rain unable to penetrate the thatch. But, all around us, the simple homes in our village were becoming a victim to the weather. Over the winter, cracks appeared in the walls; they filled with water and, as it froze, they opened further. It seemed that no one cared to make repairs. Only the farm cottages stood strong. People preferred the comfort of the town, and I wondered if one day our fragile community would be gone forever.

Shaking off these saddening thoughts, I followed my family into the cottage and placed my shawl on the metal hooks. I could see mother was weary; she hadn't said anything but her skin was pale and her eyes dull from the walk to New Romney and home again. I busied myself with preparing our mid-day meal of pottage and chunks of bread.

"I thought we could walk across the fields to Old Romney," Edmund suggested, as we left the cottage.

"It's a favourite walk of mine," I replied, my heart feeling lighter.

"There's quite a chill in the air. Will you be warm enough?"

"Aye." I took my shawl from the pegs.

"Good, Good," Edmund said as we stepped outside. He linked his arm with mine, making it awkward to negotiate the ruts in the track. It felt odd to be clamped to him in this way.

"We turn here, after the forge," I offered.

A gate needing to be opened forced us apart and Edmund resisted claiming my arm again.

"It's a pretty church, St Clement's at Old Romney," Edmund said.

"Very pretty," I agreed. And he was right, it was a lovely little church with its tower sitting beside it and partly encircled by a drainage ditch. "We'll soon be able to see it quite clearly."

The field track took us across the rough grass until we reached another wider track, bareing the signs that it was used regularly by both humans and animals. It ran beside the Wallingham Sewer, a deep, reed-lined ditch with willows on its banks.

"I can't imagine a time when this little place was of greater importance than New Romney." Edmund waved his hand in the direction of the cottages and farmhouses of Old Romney. "It had three churches, you know."

"That was when the river ran by."

"Of course," Edmund agreed. "All long gone now; they wouldn't have been stone churches you know."

"No, it was before King William, before he ordered for St Nicholas to be built." As the track turned, I looked towards a patch of ground where, even after many centuries, it seemed that the ground was a little uneven and the grass a little coarser. "They say that is the site of St Lawrence's Church."

"Do they?" He studied it for a moment, then dismissed the idea. "It would have been very small, hardly likely for any remains to still show."

It seemed, although he left the words unsaid, Edmund was again thinking of St Nicholas – that great example of Norman architecture. And as we reached, St Clements, he seemed to feel the need to compare it to the larger church in New Romney. I listened to his words and said nothing in return; he seemed to expect no more from me other than the occasional nod or murmur of agreement.

The afternoon finished with a cup of wine and some spiced cake in our cottage. When Edmund left, he took my hands in his. "How nice to spend some time with you," he said. He pressed my hands within his own, and I lowered my eyes rather than allow them to meet his and my lips remained free of his.

Jessica's Story
Chapter Three

Sunday was the day I would meet with Edmund, and we fell into a pattern of taking our mid-day meal with either his family or mine, then taking a walk together. But, for six days a week, my life continued in much the same pattern as usual, starting with an early morning walk into New Romney. My father worked at the mill and we walked into the town together, parting where our lane crossed the High Street.

The shop I worked in was on the main road through which people travelled. In the mornings, I passed the market traders setting up their stalls. There were familiar faces behind those from which fresh produce was sold, alongside the occasional ragged pedlar touting his wares. The atmosphere was lively, with people calling out and a fair amount of banter between stall-holders and customers.

On stepping through the doorway into the draper's shop, I entered a different world. Here all noise was muffled by the bales of cloth. The interior was dim, as we relied mainly on light from the front windows. Dust from the cloth hung in the air, exposed by the early morning light as it sent its shafts across the room. The well-being of a market trader was ruled by the weather but here, in the draper's, I was sheltered from the rain and the worst of the cold or heat.

The shop had a friendly atmosphere. Housewives liked to chatter as they chose their fabrics. I found it easy to talk to the local women about their families, the weather and the quality of seasonal foods. These were women whom I had known all my life and hearing their news brought variety to my day. They enjoyed a gossip, some more than others! There were a few who should have known better than to talk in such a way about their neighbours, and I tried to distance myself from any spiteful chatter.

"Have you chosen your material for the dress you'll wear on your wedding day?"

I was asked the same question again and again and my reply was well-worn: "A blue woollen cloth. Mother and I are stitching it in the evenings."

"Lucky you are to have Kate as a mother; a fine needlewoman, she is."

"I'm very lucky." And I would smile to think of my mother and the time we spent together, making those tiny stitches and deciding on the additional trims. Then my heart would sink to think of living away from home and there being no more evenings by the fireside with my parents and James.

"And what about the trimmings?" They would finger the reels of lace and ribbon, wanting to be a part of choosing the decorative details on the dress.

"Nothing too fussy," I would reply, and sense their disappointment.

"You've a fine lace shawl."

"I have," I would confirm, imagining it wrapped about my shoulders. My father had given it to me one day last summer. I didn't ask where it came from; it seemed too fine for Romney Marsh.

I didn't feel so comfortable when the salesmen from

the cloth manufacturers came into the shop. Sometimes they had to wait to be seen by the shop owner, as it was not my duty to make decisions regarding stock. I was expected to offer them refreshment as they waited. Some of these men could be a little too familiar and I was uncertain of how to respond to their coarse comments or insincere flattery. I stuttered awkward replies. As a newly betrothed woman, I had gained no confidence. Other men were perfectly polite, but what could I say to them? After they left I thought of my attempts at conversation and felt embarrassed all over again. Why could I not have said something clever or more suitable?

One afternoon we were expecting a salesman from Cranbrook. I was asked to take samples from him, as no one else was available. I was dreading this and my mouth kept drying up in anticipation of having to make conversation. I was busy tidying the bales of material, trying to keep myself occupied. There was a noise outside and I looked up to see a young man tripping as he entered the shop, falling heavily against the door frame and uttering a muffled curse as he dropped his samples of cloth. He pushed his hair out of his eyes and looked towards me as he rushed around picking them up.
"What an entrance!" he announced ruefully.
"Are you hurt?" I went to help pick up his cloth. His arrival had been so sudden and the manner of it so unexpected, there was no time for me to think of feeling uncomfortable in the presence of this stranger.
"I tripped on the loose paving; I should be more watchful," he replied. "No injuries of importance, just a bump to my hand." He held out his left hand; there was a red mark across it where it had hit the door

frame as he slipped.

"It looks sore; do you think it is broken?"

"No, I'll have a fine bruise tomorrow though. Now let me introduce myself – Ralf Radcliffe. You were expecting me?"

The conversation had started spontaneously and I forgot my fear. Mr Radcliffe was tall, but not excessively so, and of a slim build. His blue eyes lit up with enthusiasm as he talked, his skin was pale and his hair quite dark. As I looked at the samples of material, he spoke with confidence of their quality. His own clothes were made from the cloth he sold and looked very fine on him; he clearly used a good tailor.

Our conversation may have been focused on his samples of material, but my attention was held by his enthusiasm for the product he sold and his confidence I would feel the same. I felt at ease and could even offer some comments that interested him. He paid attention to me and really listened to anything I said.

"This colour suits you." Ralf Radcliffe held a piece of woollen cloth in a soft shade of green up against me, his hand lightly brushing against my cheek.. "What pretty hair you have."

This stranger made me feel attractive and I was unused to such compliments. Edmund did not believe in flattery or romantic talk and I knew that these things do not keep a house warm or a family fed. I was to be blessed with a good husband, but part of me wished he could make me feel as Ralf did on our first meeting.

I was so absorbed in our conversation and watching the expressions of animation on the salesman's face that my spirits sunk to hear someone enter the shop. It was Elinor, daughter of a local magistrate, pausing on the threshold as her eyes adjusted to the dim light. Her gown was of fine quality, her hair dark and glossy, her eyes a vivid blue.

"I've come to collect Mother's silk." Elinor stepped forward, casting her eyes over Mr Radcliffe. In return his appraisal of her clearly showed appreciation of her beauty.

"Of course." I turned and reached for the package. I was jolted back to reality, to a life where Jessica has nothing of interest to say, is less attractive and lacking in knowledge of the world beyond Romney Marsh. Feeling uncomfortable in Elinor's presence, my cheeks burned for ever thinking I could speak with Ralf Radcliffe and hold his interest.

Then Elinor was gone and he was still there, but the ease I felt in his company had passed. Ralf concentrated on tidying away his samples and still spoke to me as he did so. My replies were awkward and dull.

"It was a pleasure to meet such a charming young woman today and I look forward to seeing you again at the end of the week. I do hope we can tempt you to stock our cloth," he concluded.

"Thank you for your time." I forced the words out. "Your cloth is of good quality and I'm sure we'll buy some. Good afternoon."

I opened the shop door and watched him walk down the street, towards the inn where his horse was stabled. His head was held high and after several long strides he turned to give me a farewell wave.

The week continued much the same as any other. I had little time to spend on fanciful thoughts, but occasionally an image of Ralf's sparkling eyes, and the memory of enthusiasm in his voice entered my mind. I tried to ignore it, for this was disloyal to Edmund, the man Father had chosen for me.

I am ashamed to say that, despite my resolve not to think of Ralf, I found myself looking forward to his next visit. I so wanted him to admire me and remembered how dowdy I felt when the beautiful Elinor entered the shop. I bought a hair clip and told myself it would look pretty to wear for church on a Sunday. In the evenings I altered a dress; it had never fitted very well before. On the day I was to see Ralf I wore the dress and the hair clip.

"You're looking pretty today, Jessica," Mother said, as she ladled porridge. "Have you changed your hair?"

"It's nothing much," I replied. "I altered this dress a little and the hair clip came from a stall on the High Street."

"The dress hangs better now," Mother remarked, standing back to look at it.

"Will you be seeing Edmund today?" James asked.

"I don't know." I sat down and started eating, not wanting the attention on myself.

Before leaving for work, I returned to my small bedroom under the thatched roof and removed the hair clip. I would wear it on Sunday, and have no thoughts of this other young man.

Yet I found it hard to concentrate on my work and when Ralf Radcliffe entered the shop, I felt the colour rise in my cheeks.

"Good morning, no dramatic entrance from me today!" He laughed and his words put me at ease.

"I trust you had a good journey."

"Tedious, but worthwhile I hope."

I pulled the samples on to the huge table where we usually spread the cloth, then picked out the materials my employer wanted to buy. "He'll try these three to start with and perhaps more later." I looked at Ralf, hoping he would not be disappointed. "We have very little spare space."

"That is fine," Ralf replied. "I have other orders in Lydd, Dymchurch, Hythe and Folkstone. My time here is not wasted." He held up the square of the fine woollen material in a soft green. "I see you have chosen to stock this one. Will you take my advice and buy some for yourself? It would suit you very well." Ralf looked straight into my eyes and smiled.

His words made me blush and I concentrated on the cloth, so as to avoid his gaze. "I think I shall; it's a pretty colour."

"Good, and perhaps some time I will see you wearing it; I'm sure it will be in great demand when the women see how lovely it looks on you."

"Oh, I...."

"Well, I must thank you for your business and hope your customers like the cloth."

"And will it be you delivering the cloth, in a month or so, you said?"

"I will make sure of it." Then he was gone, having flashed a smile as he stepped out on to the street.

That afternoon my thoughts kept dwelling on the time I spent with Ralf. I had never experienced this type of attention from a man before and was surprised to find that I was vain enough to enjoy it. How easily a normally sensible young woman can have her head turned by a little flattery!

Reality returned with a jolt when I left work that afternoon and saw Edmund strolling down the street towards me. Colour flooded my face as he approached me; my traitorous thoughts were plain for him to see, I was sure of it. Shame cloaked me, as I saw the man my father had chosen for me.

"Jessica, how pleasant to see you, very pleasant."

"Edmund, good afternoon. Are you well?" I put my hands on my cheeks to cool them.

"Oh aye, you will find that I keep myself in good health." He smiled and nodded, clearly pleased with himself. "How is your father?"

"He is well. I am about to meet him at the mill."

"Splendid, splendid. You look a little flushed Jessica," Edmund stated without concern.

"It has been a humid day," I replied, avoiding his gaze.

"My mother says that she looks forward to seeing you again on Sunday and you don't need to tell me that a service at St Nicholas will be a welcome change for your family." He glanced towards the church tower, just seen above the rooftops. "Well, I will not keep you, your father will be waiting. Good afternoon, Jessica."

Living in our remote village, there were few chances to be entertained and so, if there were an opportunity to travel into New Romney for a show or fair, I was keen to be a part of it. News came that the Hythe Players were to perform in the town and it had been arranged that James, Ellen, Nathan and I would go together to see the performance.

But, as a betrothed woman, was it my place to go with my friends and family, or should I be a part of Edmund's family group? I knew that Edmund disapproved of these shows and my usual pleasure was shadowed with concern

"I wasn't sure if I should go," I said to Ellen.

"Why ever not?" she asked.

"It's Edmund. He disapproves of these performances; the subject can be crude and immoral. I wouldn't like to disappoint him."

"The play is about St George and the dragon," Ellen replied. "I'm sure there is no harm in it and if your father allows it then it is for him to say." We were in the dairy as I was collecting milk and butter for my family. She wiped her hands on her apron and returned to the butter churn. "It's for you to decide; I do hope you'll come."

I fidgeted with my shawl, thinking of the simple pleasure gained from the travelling entertainment and the joy on James' face as he watched them. "I should hate to upset Edmund. I'm sure he has good reason to dislike these plays. You'll be married one day and understand a man likes his wife to respect his opinions."

"I understand," Ellen said. But it seemed to me that Ellen didn't worry as I did, that she would smile and laugh her way through life.

"I'll come this time... I think...," I said.

"I'm hoping Bertie will be there," Ellen confided. "Bertie from the forge, you know."

"Aye, I know! You mention him often enough." I felt myself relax a little. "I'm sure he will be there and perhaps pleased to join us for a while."

Two days later, James and I met with Nathan and Ellen, who had been waiting at the end of the farm track. Many people from the neighbouring area were also making their way to New Romney; it was a treat to have an evening out and the atmosphere was merry. As we neared the outskirts of the town music could be heard. Voices were raised as revellers called out to each other. Food was being cooked over fires; the aroma filled the air and made our mouths water.

On the green a stage was set on a cart. The players had pulled it from Hythe, stopping at

Dymchurch to perform and would continue on their way tomorrow. A cloth hung from the back of the stage to depict a countryside scene. Someone called out to announce the entertainment was about to begin and the audience made their way forward. The wealthy were able to hire a seat, so as not to muddy their clothes. Some had carried their own tables and chairs through the town and set up a feast to enjoy as they watched the show. We laid a cloth on the ground, to save our clothes from the worst of the dirt.

There was a hush as the first of the players stepped up on to the stage. From the side, a description of the scene was given and the characters were introduced. The story of St George and the dragon was a popular one and the audience shouted out their encouragement.

During an interval there was the opportunity to refresh ourselves with ale or wine and freshly cooked meat with bread. It was then that Bertie joined us.

"Would you care for some bread and bacon?" he asked Ellen.

"Aye, that would be good," she replied and, looking back at us, she continued: "I'll go with Bertie and be back in a while."

James and I followed, the smells were tempting and we didn't want to miss out. It seemed as if Ellen's romance would go smoothly for her, that she needn't wait for her father to find her a husband, I reflected. I admit to feeling a little jealous; how foolish when my father had found me a good husband.

The call came for the play to continue. We sat, still feeling the warmth of the sun on our backs as it descended towards the horizon. The winter was now far behind us and warm weather encouraged us to enjoy times, like this evening with the Hythe Players.

Jessica's Story
Chapter Four

The weather had been dry, as it often is in August. Just two weeks before the wedding, a fierce summer storm raged around us. It darkened the skies and caused the wind to force its way through the gaps in the window frames. As we ate our supper the storm raged above us, thunder and lightning coming simultaneously. The rain was torrential and we were thankful that the wind was not driving water down our chimney.

The sounds of the storm were joined by a rhythmic banging noise somewhere outside. The wind buffeted something, perhaps a fallen branch or open door. Then, as we finished our meal, there came another sound, as if someone were rapping on the door.

"Who could that be?" Father got up from the table.

We all turned to face the kitchen door, waiting to see who had braved the storm to call on us. It was our neighbour, John, who was ushered into the kitchen. Even the short step between our homes had given the rain enough opportunity to soak his outer clothes. He was clearly agitated.

"What a night for it to happen.... It's my mother, she's taken a bad turn, we fear for the worst. Please, Clement, would you go for the parson? Mary is with her, but I don't like to leave."

"Of course. James, my coat, please." Father was ready to help his friend and neighbour.

"Thank you, now I must..." John turned back to the door.

"You get back there straight away, and if there is anything we can do, you need only to ask." Mother gave his damp arm a reassuring pat and then he was gone. Uncle Clement followed him out of the door.

We were all rather quiet as we tidied away after the meal. The old woman had been ill for a while and the news was expected, but still a shock. Moving into the parlour, Mother lit candles but they fluttered frantically in the draughts. The light was too poor for us to work on the fine stitching around the hem of my wedding dress. I felt unsettled, picking up the material and looking at our stitching then replacing it and looking from the window at the driving rain.

Father returned with the news: "The parson is there; all we can do is wait for the news. I fear the morning will bring word that she is no longer with us on this Earth."

Not long after, I knelt on the bare floorboards beside my bed and muttered a prayer for the dying woman's soul.

The storm continued on its way. Thunder became a distant grumble and the rain lessened. By morning the sky was a bright blue, clouds moving lazily across the sky. The land had welcomed the rainfall and the fields were all the greener for it. The dust had been washed off the walls of the cottages and everything looked brighter and cleaner. It was a beautiful day. That morning I lingered at the window, lifting my eyes up towards the distant hills, a purple band where the Marsh ended.

We were eating breakfast when there was a knock on the front door. It was rare for us to have visitors and we assumed it would be our neighbour, John, with news of his mother. But to our surprise the visitor was ushered into the other room. We were none the wiser as to who it was, a male voice being the only clue.

"Who could that be? Why didn't Father bring him in here?" James asked with indignation.

"We don't know any more than you do. Now eat up your breakfast and all you can do is wait and see like the rest of us," Mother told him, while she cut up the last of yesterday's bread.

"It's probably nothing of interest," I commented, keen to pacify my brother.

It must have been five or ten minutes later when my uncle led a man into the kitchen. He looked familiar: a short, stocky man. But I couldn't place him; certainly he was not from our village. Both the stranger and my father looked uneasy, as if reluctant to say anything. No one spoke for a few seconds. They were looking at me, and I felt a chill pass through my body. My mother saw it too, and came to my side, placing her hand on the small of my back.

"This is Edmund's uncle," Father told us. Of course, now I saw the family likeness. Father continued, his voice hesitant; he did not want to be the one to give the news. "There is no easy way to tell you this... Edmund... he was out in the storm last night and was crushed... crushed by a falling branch of a tree as it was hit by lightning. Jessica, my dear, he was badly injured and could not be saved."

"So sudden," the uncle said. "It was a delivery, you see. From the shop. One that had been missed earlier and he knew it needed doing."

"What a terrible... a terrible thing to happen," It

seemed as if Mother had to force the words out. "A sad loss." She moved closer to me and I stood there, not knowing how to respond. Edmund, my betrothed... Edmund whom I was planning to marry in just over a week's time... had been killed by a falling tree. A tree, not a whole tree, we learnt. No, he was killed by a branch of a tree as it fell to the ground.

How was I meant to feel or react? What should I say to the man, the uncle who stood there beside Father? The stranger opened his mouth a few times, scratched at his beard and looked as if he had something to say, but was not quite sure of how to say it. He just stood there, as we all did, unsure how to react.

"I'm sorry, Jess," my father said, and looked towards my mother for support and guidance.

I managed to say some words to Edmund's uncle: "I can't quite believe it; we are... were... to be married in two weeks... and now he is gone. It was good of you to remember me at a time like this. I appreciate your coming... coming to tell me."

"It's a shock to us all; some terrible things happen to good men," Edmund's uncle replied.

"Aye, he was a good man and will be sorely missed by his family," my father offered.

"Please pass on our condolences to your family." Mother then offered refreshments and we were all secretly relieved when he declined.

Then the uncle was gone; there was nothing else to be said, other than repeat the same sentiments. I sat close to the fire, trying to draw some warmth from it. Father left for work; I would remain at home for the day. Left to my own thoughts, while all around me everyday life continued. After a while, James went to his lessons with the parson and Mother sat at the table preparing bread dough. Then it came to me – the place I should be and I stood, perhaps abruptly.

"I must go to the church to pray for his soul," I announced.

"I will go with you, my dear," Mother went to clean the flour from her hands.

"No, no, I am happy to go alone."

I sought refuge in the church, sitting on the wooden bench, watching the dust motes dance in the narrow beams of light coming through the high lancet windows. I tried to pray for Edmund's soul, but mostly my thoughts were on the ordeals ahead of me: the painful meeting with his family and the funeral. It was cool in the church and, eventually, my thoughts settled. I felt comforted by the peace. I don't know how long I sat, but in the end I knew I must go home.

That afternoon I went with my mother and father, who had left work early, to visit the Blackstock family.

"Here she is, our Jessica," Mr Blackstock's voice lacked his usual confidence.

"I'm sorry... I can't... such a shock." My words were inadequate and it was my parents who spoke for me.

We stayed for a short time, perhaps only twenty minutes, and left feeling great pity for his mother and sisters who wept and his father who spoke of his son's great virtues.

"You'll come again, Jessica. Soon. You'll come and be with us again soon," Mrs Blackstock clawed at my sleeve.

"Of course," I replied, trying to avoid her gaze.

"It will become easier, Jess." My father said as we walked away from their shop. "In time, their grief will be less desperate. Less demanding on yourself."

I prayed long and hard for both Edmund and, selfishly, for guidance and support for myself at this time. What was my future now? Shocked and confused by his death, I could barely admit to myself that I didn't feel the loss of my betrothed.

The funeral was planned and was to be just days before the date when we should have married. I focussed on the texture of the ancient stone walls and the carved pillars; the gentle light cast on them through plain glass windows. How many funerals had these walls seen over the centuries? The priest said how sorry he was that he would no longer be marrying Edmund and myself; I felt everyone turn slightly towards me and I hung my head, wondering how I was supposed to feel about a man I barely knew. I feel ashamed at my lack of regret as I stood there for Edmund's funeral rather than for our wedding.

It was at this time of mixed emotions, as we stood at the graveside, that I next saw Ralf Radcliffe. He had not been in the shop for about a month and I had resolved not to think of him, keeping myself busy with preparation for my life with Edmund. But suddenly, there he was, standing just beyond the churchyard wall; how strange he should appear on the day of Edmund's funeral.

I concentrated on speaking with Mrs Blackstock and her daughters; they could barely control their grief. Uncomfortable in their presence, I felt like an outsider looking in. It was a relief when my parents joined us and were able to support me.

"Jessica... Jess, come along." My father gently placed his hand on my arm. "We'll walk together." The family and close friends began to meander through the churchyard, towards the Blackstocks' home where we were to share a meal and wine.

I looked over to where Ralf had stood; he had gone. For what reason would he loiter at the churchyard at such a time? I looked again. If he had been there, it would have made no difference as there could not possibly be any conversation between us. He must have had shops to visit and material to sell, and would now be on his way home.

The summer passed and there is little of interest to write in Anna's notebooks. My life returned to its previous patterns. The wedding dress was put away in a trunk, just as Anna's had been. In fact, it is only as I write that I now reflect on how our lives followed a similar path: both of us due to marry and both losing our betrothed within days of the wedding. Yet, whereas Anna mourned for her love who was very much alive, I could only feel shameful relief that mine lay wrapped in a shroud of linen, with the dried leaves of rosemary and lavender.

I was once more a daughter, sister and plain Jessica. As the leaves turned to all shades of yellow, orange and brown, I struggled to see what the future would hold. The harvest festival passed and the long winter months loomed. In our row of roadside cottages, we remained the only home occupied. Our neighbours on both sides had left and no new families wanted to move to our remote settlement. They preferred to live in the towns or larger villages, and I could understand that there was nothing left in Hope to tempt them here – not even a cottage, with three rooms and a good roof of reed thatch.

By the time November came, the long hot summer was a distant memory. We were absorbed in the struggle to keep warm, dry and well nourished over the winter months. James worked hard to collect a stock of firewood that would fuel the fires over the next few months. In the garden, vegetables were picked and stored in a dry place or preserved. The days began and ended in cold, damp darkness as they grew shorter. It was as if we had all slipped back in time, as my own life continued in the same pattern as before Edmund came into it. Perhaps not quite the same... I felt a little older and maybe wiser.

The winter of 1587 was a hard one, with many weeks of the frost lying on the ground and times when the road to New Romney was impassable with snow. We huddled around the fire in our cottage, thankful that James had collected a good pile of wood over the summer months. As the chill of winter began to ease, I saw my mother was wearier than ever and feared for her health. The Marsh Fever, which she had succumbed to when I was a child, frequently tormented her with a recurrence of the sweating sickness and we constantly dreaded its return.

One day I returned from work to find Mother was not in the cottage. She had taken advantage of the thaw in order to walk across the fields to see her sister in Old Romney, but when she returned I saw her skin was grey and she seemed barely able to walk across the room before slumping in the chair before the fire.

"I've stayed near the home for so long, and the journey was more tiring than I thought, with the thaw making the ground so slippery." She smiled up at me, but her eyes were dulled. "It's nothing to concern you, Jess. But if you wouldn't mind preparing the supper I would be grateful."

"Of course, Mother." I pulled on an apron.

"James, would you please check on the chickens," Mother asked.

With James busy in the garden I took the

opportunity to press her further: "Is it the Marsh Fever? I know how you hate to complain, but if I can do anything to help..."

"I'm still feeling rather tired, Jessica," Mother admitted.

"Then I must do more to help, perhaps I could finish work a little earlier to be here with you?"

"No, I must manage. It is not the fever, but there is something though – something so unexpected – James was eleven last February. Jess, I am to have another baby."

"Oh Mother!" I tried to sound happy but there were always risks with pregnancy. My mother was neither young nor healthy.

"You are not a child and we can talk of these things. God has chosen to bless me with a baby and I pray that all will be well. I suffer from a little indigestion and the tiredness of course.

"When is it due?"

"Towards the end of June; in three months' time."

"Then I'll help you prepare. What a surprise! I'll pray for a healthy brother or sister and a speedy delivery." My words belied the fear I felt for both my mother and the unborn child.

Jessica's Story
Chapter Five

In February, a letter came from father's sister, who lived in a town called Rye, some hours away by horse. My cousin, who was about a year older than myself, was to be married. We were all invited. I studied the letter; my aunt's writing was large and bold, sweeping across the page.

"The roads will still be in poor condition; it won't be an easy journey," my father said thoughtfully.

"But, Father, we must go!" James cried out.

"You go, but I couldn't possibly." Mother laid a hand over the gentle swell of her stomach. "It would be too tiring."

"Then I should perhaps stay?" I said, although my heart sank.

Rye was a place of great mystery to me: a hill-top town almost surrounded by the sea and three rivers, one of those rivers being our own long-gone Rother, which had once flowed past Hope, before changing its course during the thirteenth-century storms. Said to be encased by town walls, with gateways, cobbled streets and topped with a church, the town was known for its battles with the French.

Stifled by long months of being forced to huddle at the fireside, or scurry from place to place as icy air nipped at bare skin and stabbed through layers of woollen clothing, I had a sudden longing for an adventure. I imagined my senses coming alive with the noises of a bustling town, the scents of the sea and the cooking pots containing spices from far-off lands. And how I would enjoy seeing the people of that town and the buildings jostling for position on the crowded hillside.

"We'll go, the three of us," my father stated.

"Can we really?" I asked, still hardly daring to hope.

"I'd like to see my sister again, if it's possible." Father looked towards Mother and she gave a slight nod.

"I won't go… the journey will tire me," Mother said. "But you must and when you return, I'll hear all your tales."

"Perhaps I should stay here, with you?" I turned to mother

"No Jess, you must go and think nothing of me. You work hard and it doesn't go unnoticed." Mother reached forward and laid her hand on my arm. "It would make me very happy to know you have been to see your family and a new place."

"But how will we get there?" James asked, eyes wide and cheeks flushed with excitement. "The river, how will we cross it?"

"We'll borrow a horse and cart, perhaps from Farmer Farley, and there is sure to be an inn or a farm where we can leave it before we cross the river," Father replied. "It will be dependent on the tides of course."

"Crossing the river?" I queried.

"It's tidal," Father said, frowning as if trying to recall it from a time when he once visited the town, crossing the river by boat and travelling from Kent into Sussex.

We rose early in the morning on the last Saturday of March. Our bags were already packed. Mother cut chunks of fresh bread to go with cheese, fruit and a jug of ale during the journey. Nathan Farley brought the farm horse and cart to our cottage and Father lifted our bags into the cart. The weather looked to be fair and we hoped for a good journey. We left while the land was still wet with dew and the early mists hung in soft swathes, taking Mother's love with us.

We journeyed first to Ivychurch, a village of no great size, but with a church no smaller than that of St Nicholas in New Romney. The cluster of mud and thatch cottages, the forge, the pub, were all familiar to me. We passed farm labourers and saw women at the village pump, recognising many of them and calling out a greeting. Then Ivychurch was behind us and we turned towards the west, travelling for several miles along a narrow road, with a drainage ditch to one side. We passed very few buildings and, other than the sheep in the fields, there was little sign of life.

Passing through Brenzett, another small place far from the coast or any town, we travelled on to Brookland where we stopped at the roadside and were grateful to step down from the cart. Here my curiosity was stirred by the very odd church tower. Not that I had seen many towers in my life, having travelled no further than Dymchurch in one direction and Brenzett in the other. This one was shaped like a cone, and covered in wooden shingles.

"How could they build a tower of stone on this church?" Father replied to my questioning. "The ground had been drained, but to build on it was a risk. Here, there were wide channels with the sea flowing inland and always the fear of the earth banks not being able to hold it back. The village was vulnerable to the sea, in the times when this land was drained. Then to put a heavy tower on the church..."

"It would have fallen and taken the church with it," James said, and I saw his eyes light up as he imagined the scene, with villagers scattering in panic and the church a forlorn ruin.

We ate some of our bread and cheese and wandered around the churchyard, before returning to the cart and moving the reluctant horse away from the lush grass she had found. The road continued, and at one point we travelled higher up, on top of an ancient sea defence. The great mud bank continued towards the sea and we turned again, now looking for our first glimpse of Rye's church on top of its island hill.

But if we thought Brookland church was unusual with its wooden cone-tower, how strange it was to see an odd box-shaped brick church with a flat roof. This was as we crossed into Sussex and the cluster of cottages known as East Guldeford.

"It looks like a barn, but not even a barn has a great flat roof," I mused. "I wonder why… is this how churches are in Sussex?"

"We'll see soon enough," Father replied. "But I recall the church in Rye had a roof just like those we are used to."

Here, at East Guldeford, we spoke to a villager who directed us to Salts Farm, where the pony and cart could be left for the next two days. Father had already consulted the fishermen of New Romney and we knew the river was safe to cross at that time, so the three of us walked to the bank of the tidal inlet and, as we watched the ferry boat approach from Rye, it seemed that our adventure was truly beginning.

"Head up through the Landgate," the ferryman said,

waving his hand in the direction of a pair of ancient rounded stone towers with an opening between them. Houses butted up against the yellowed stone, becoming part of the town wall. "You were wanting the Mermaid – up the hill and ask anyone, they'll all be able to point the way."

"Thank you." Father placed some coins in the man's rough hand and we moved aside to let a pair of young farm labourers take their turn in the boat.

We picked up our bags and walked along the cobbled street, until we were in the shadow of the great Landgate. Passing under it, we continued, finding the road was steep, unlike any on Romney Marsh. After a few minutes, we paused and looked at the view: below us the sea was breaking on the rocks, and beyond it was a wide estuary with mudflats and numerous channels. The air was damp and salty, the shrill cry of the sea-birds mingling with the sounds of a busy town.

Walking up the hill, we stopped frequently to exclaim over the view, and then the town's buildings were on either side of us and we had other things to see. Now we were among the shops with their wares displayed outside: the butcher, the wine merchant, the drapers, the baker – they were all there. The street was busy as it was still mid-afternoon. Boys led animals on pieces of rope, housewives carried baskets, men pushed carts and children scattered before them all. We picked our way over the cobbles, alert to the sounds and smells of this old town.

"We're looking for the Mermaid Inn; could you direct us?" Father paused before a fresh-faced woman with a shopping basket held before her.

"I thought you were newcomers." She looked us up and down and continued, "See just along there, the tall, narrow house facing the road? Well, take the road opposite and at the end turn right. You'll not miss the Mermaid, its quite a size and there'll be all manner of people coming and going."

"Thank you." Father gave a nod and we continued on our way.

"Welcome to the Mermaid. Now, let me guess, you must be the ones who are here for Harry Tanner's wedding to his Lizzie." The plump landlady looked very pleased with herself; her eyes twinkled and her smiles were infectious.

"He is to wed my niece," my father replied.

"A fine young couple, they are. Now, Bob can help you with those bags and I bet you're hungry." She turned and called: "Bob, Bob, out of that chair – there's bags to be carried."

"Thank you. We'd be glad of a hot meal," Father replied.

"My daughter will bring you up some water so you can clean away the dirt from the roads. Take some time to settle in, then come down to eat. There's a room away from that rabble at the bar – how does that suit?" The landlady turned again. "*Bob*, do you hear me?"

Bob appeared from his chair, the bar or wherever he had been. He gave a grunt and a nod and picked up our bags in his strong arms. Stooping to avoid low beams, he set off up the stairs and we followed. At the end of a corridor he opened the doors to two rooms and placed our belongings in them. We thanked him and he gave another grunt of acknowledgement before leaving.

My room faced towards the back yard of the pub; through the thick glass at the window I could just see the movement of horses. It was small, furnished only with two beds, a table and cupboard for clothes. The walls were whitewashed, the single decoration being a painting depicting a religious scene.

I felt weary after the journey and perhaps a little emotional when I thought of Mother left behind on her own. But a splash of water on my face and a brush through my hair left me eager to see more of Rye and the Mermaid Inn. Soon we were eating a hearty fish soup with chunks of bread. We sat alone in the small parlour; the noise from the bar could be heard nearby.

The evening was spent in the home of my uncle and aunt, whom I barely remembered from their visit to Hope many years beforehand. My cousin, Lizzie, was there and I found myself liking her very much. As I grew comfortable in their presence I was able to ask questions about their home town and the man, Harry Tanner, who was to marry Lizzie the following day. Too soon darkness had set in and my uncle walked us back along unfamiliar streets to the Mermaid Inn.

How strange it was to wake to the sounds of a town: hooves and wheels on the cobbles, the calls of delivery boys, the movement of people in the busy inn. My sleep had been fitful as you would expect, although the straw mattress was comfortable enough.

The following morning I dressed quickly in the skirt and bodice of fine wool that I was to wear for the wedding. Having added ribbons to my hair, and pinned my lace shawl with a brooch, I pulled on my shoes. Then I walked along the hallway of the inn and tapped on the door of the room where my father and James had spent the night.

Breakfast was eaten to the accompaniment of church bells. They reminded us that we needed to hurry if we were to be in time to see the wedding vows exchanged in the church porch. We had taken a walk the previous afternoon and found St Mary's Church, so knew which of the narrow streets to take as we scurried along in our best clothes.

The townspeople were all walking in the same direction. As newcomers we attracted some glances but this was a town where foreign merchants often came as well as visitors from the surrounding villages, so strangers were nothing out of the ordinary. On our way we passed timber-framed houses all butted up, one against the other. Finally we stepped into the churchyard.

St Mary's was a thick-set building, with flying buttresses and a squat tower. Approaching the porch from the street, it seemed to have very little land around it. However, we knew from our walk the previous evening that there was a small churchyard to the far side. On nearing the building, we stepped aside, allowing others to pass inside. We wanted to see my cousin marry at the church porch, before continuing the wedding service within the church.

Over the next few minutes, other church-goers stepped off the path and paused outside the porch. We exchanged smiles and greetings, knowing them to be there for the same reason.

"Good morrow, Clement, Jessica, James." It was my uncle, with cousin Lizzie.

"Good day," I smiled at Lizzie. She wore a pretty dress of blue linen and her dark hair was threaded with spring flowers.

"Were you comfortable at the Mermaid?" Lizzie asked.

"We were – although to be in a town…it's so very different."

"Noisier, I imagine," Lizzie replied. "It was good to

meet you yesterday, cousin Jessica. My mother tells me we met when we were still in napkins, but I have no memory of it."

"Neither do I, but I am told this is not my first visit to Rye. What an interesting town."

"It certainly is, although I imagine the open countryside brings its own interest."

"Here comes Harry," my uncle announced, and we all turned to see a group of young men approaching.

The priest stepped forward from the porch, extending his arms outwards, inviting the young couple to move towards him. With a glance towards her father, Lizzie moved with him to the porch. At the same time, Harry Tanner joined them and his hand reached out to take Lizzie's. They exchanged a smile. *It seems to be a love match*, I thought. *I am happy for them for she seems like a good woman and someone I would like to call my friend, if only we lived closer.*

"Gather near, family and friends of this young couple," the priest said. "Listen to their vows before we step inside." He paused for a moment as we moved forward and then continued. "We are here today to see the union between Harry Tanner and Lizzie Browning of this parish. Harry, do you take Lizzie in marriage?"

"I will," Harry replied.

"And Lizzie, do you take Harry in marriage?"

"I do," she replied, looking at Harry.

"The rings?" The priest looked towards another young man, possibly a brother or cousin of Harry's. He handed the gold bands to the priest who then placed them on a bible. "Bless, O Lord these rings, as a sign of the solemn vows by which these two people have bound themselves to each other in this Holy Covenant, through Jesus Christ our Lord, Amen."

The rings were then placed on the fourth finger of the left hand and, with their fingers linked together, Harry and Lizzie followed the priest into the church. We fell in step behind them. Over the noise of the townsfolk already gathered in the church, the rise and fall of the priest's voice could be heard as he recited a psalm. We slipped onto empty benches and watched as the couple were led to the altar. Here they knelt and were covered with a veil while a prayer was offered. When the veil was lifted and they rose to their feet, Harry and Lizzie were married and were once more blessed before moving to sit with the rest of the congregation.

The church service began, and I went through the motions of following it, but my thoughts were on my future. It was now a year since Father had arranged my betrothal with Edmund. I had avoided thinking about another marriage, concentrating only on my relief in being free of him. Now I feared my cousin's wedding would bring his thoughts back to finding a husband for me.

We returned to the Mermaid Inn, a rambling tavern stretching out along the road and with many additional rooms at the rear. It was larger than any hostelry in Romney and was sizeable enough to welcome the wedding party within its ancient walls. The evening before my father, James and I had eaten in a small parlour, now we were in a large, heavily beamed room with the landlord smiling broadly behind the oak panelled bar and serving girls offering trays of steaming pies.

We seated ourselves on a bench and were soon joined by others from the wedding group. They made a friendly crowd and the occasion reminded me of the times when our own village gathered to celebrate an occasion such as Midsummer's eve or Christmas. I sipped on weak ale and used my fingers to pull apart the pie, revealing meat and vegetables within it. A pleasant hour or so passed, and I found the women of Rye to be friendly, with my cousin's friends curious to learn about her family from the Marsh.

Eventually my uncle, standing to draw attention to himself, called out: "Come on, William, let us hear your fiddle."

"And you, Jack, bring out your whistle," another man said.

"And do we have a tambourine?" the fiddler asked.

"Aye, I'm coming." A scrawny young man pushed his way through the guests.

"Clear the tables aside then." From the bar, the landlord waved his arm towards the crowded space.

I found myself having to move from the bench as tables were pushed to the side of the room, and an area of the floor was made clear for dancing. Musicians stood to the side of the bar and the fiddler began, the others joining in as they recognised the tune. Lizzie and her new husband were the first to dance. Soon the dancers were jostling for position in the small space and there was much merriment about the room. I didn't dance but stood against the panelled wall with my ale in my hand. Occasionally I found my foot was tapping away to the rhythm of the music.

Long after the sun had set, the guests began to tire and those who danced did so with less vigour. People had supped their limit of wine or ale and serving women cleared away the remaining food. The fire smouldered in the grate and benches were now moved so we could rest upon them. People sat in their groups chatting quietly. Children had been taken home to bed long ago and a couple of elderly men snoozed in the corner.

After a while my aunt beckoned to the young women present and said: "People are tiring now and some will have to travel home. Shall we prepare Lizzie for bed?"

How I had dreaded the thought of this moment when I had prepared for my own wedding. Why did we have this humiliating tradition of the wedding guests crowding into the bedroom to give advice and best wishes to the newly weds? Was it not embarrassing enough for a young woman to be faced with being alone with her new husband? Often the couple barely knew each other. I am ashamed to say that when I heard of Edmund's death one of my first thoughts was that I wouldn't have to suffer this public initiation.

Trailing behind the group of women, we walked back towards the church and turned into an alleyway. My aunt opened the door of a narrow house and we traipsed into the living area, then opened a door to reveal a wooden staircase.

Upstairs, the bed was decorated with flowers and ears of corn; the latter represented fertility. Someone held up Lizzie's night-shift. It was linen, with lace embroidery. I hung back, feeling uncomfortable about preparing the bride for her husband.

"Let us help you into this pretty night gown."

"Share out your ribbons; they'll bring some luck to these girls!"

"A fine young man that Harry Tanner is, if you change your mind..."

I glanced at another young woman; she looked a little embarrassed too. We exchanged an awkward smile. Lizzie was soon in her night-shift. The women shared out the ribbons from her hair and dress; some were pushed into my hand.

"I hear the men coming!"

"Harry is on his way. I'll bet you can't wait!"

Lizzie feigned embarrassment. There was a loud cheer as the door opened and Harry was pushed forward. Men who were sober enough to manage the stairs were close behind. They crowded into the room and I found myself jostled by strangers and pushed against a cupboard.

"Well, Lizzie, you're as pretty as I could wish for," Harry smiled at his new wife.

"Thank you." Lizzie bowed her head but there was a broad smile on her face.

"Get on with it! Give her a kiss," one of the men shouted.

A couple of women gestured for Lizzie to sit on the bed.

"I am sure we can manage on our own now," Harry told the enthusiastic crowd. He drew the curtains around the bed.

Jessica's Story
Chapter Six

We returned to Romney Marsh the day after the wedding. The journey seemed lengthy and we were chilled as the wind blew from the north-east. What a relief finally to reach the familiarity of Ivychurch and then to see the spire of our own dear little church at Hope. Home at last.

Mother came to the door of our cottage when she heard us arrive and we were soon standing in front of the kitchen fire, enveloped by the warmth. A stew bubbled away in a pot above the flames and smelt delicious.

"Come and warm yourselves with a hot drink and settle down by the fire; you can tell me all about it." Mother placed mugs in our hands and gestured to the stools by the hearth. "Then we can all sit down to a meal."

"We had a wonderful time, Mother. Imagine going on a boat across to Rye and all those houses squashed on a hillside." James may have been weary, but there was so much to tell.

"And what of Lizzie, how was she?"

"She looked very pretty, Mother. She wore a blue linen and Harry had a tunic to match," I told her. "And they have a small house near the church."

"James, will you fetch the plates, please?" Mother

prepared to serve the meal. "I'm so pleased to hear it went well. Tell me, were you made welcome?"

We gave Mother all the details, James interrupting, then Father or I correcting him. Finally, she was satisfied that she had been told all that she needed to know about our journey, the accommodation and, most importantly, the wedding day.

"I wish I could have been there to see Lizzie. It may be that they never come here; what do townsfolk want with this bleak Marsh?" Mother rose to start clearing the table, but her body sagged and she moved slowly. I motioned for her to sit back down.

"You'd have found the journey tedious; the chill was unbearable at times." Father spoke with concern. "We must look after your health and pray for strength over the coming months."

"Of course, I'd not have wanted you worrying over me." Her face was lined and eyes heavy but my mother gave a brave smile. "James, would you please check on the chickens whilst your father draws some water from the well?"

Not having seen my mother for several days it seemed that her weariness was more apparent. The weather had been mild and I would have expected her to be looking healthier. With James busy in the garden I took the opportunity to ask if she was feeling unwell.

"I'm still feeling rather tired, Jessica," Mother admitted.

"Was it the fever, or the baby? I should have stayed with you."

"No, you are young and must go out and enjoy yourself. God has chosen to bless me with a baby and I will take good care of myself and the little one. I suffer from a little indigestion and the tiredness of course, but think of the joy a baby will bring!"

I went to bed early that night and welcomed the familiar comfort. There was silence outside, other than the occasional bleating of the lambs. Sleep eluded me and, with the wedding so fresh in my mind, it was impossible not to wonder about what the future had in store for me.

With the roads in such poor condition over the winter, there was generally little travel between towns. In the drapery shop, stocks of material were running low and we waited for the warmer weather to bring with it the travelling salesmen with their selections of cloth. As trade began to get busier and the shelves were filled I often wondered if Ralf would be returning to our small town. He was one of the last to call.

"What poor state the roads are in on the Romney Marsh, but now I see the journey was worthwhile!" There he was, a bundle of samples under his arm. I blushed to hear those words and my heart leapt as the colour rose on my cheeks.

"This is a surprise."

"A welcome one, I hope!"

"We are in need of more cloth." I was not practised in making flirtatious comments and hoped he understood that I was truly pleased to see him.

"I'm glad about that, for I am in the business of selling cloth! However, I was meaning that it is a pleasure to see you again after the long winter. I was fretting for the roads to be good enough to make it possible for me to travel here." He was bold to speak in that way; Ralf clearly had confidence in his attraction for me.

"It is good to see you; I wondered when you would be travelling this way again."

"Because you are in need of material?" This was

accompanied with a cheeky grin.

"Of course!" Another blush as I spoke and hoped that in the dim light it would go unnoticed.

"My father recommends I stay in this area for a week in order to visit many shops. I suggested New Romney would be the ideal location, and from here I shall travel to Lydd, Hythe and Dymchurch to sell my cloth. It's an excellent arrangement, don't you agree?" Ralf smiled with satisfaction as he told of his plan.

"You are to stay for the whole week! It's generally good to see a new face in town."

"I am glad to hear you say that, for I had hoped that you might be free to meet me tomorrow afternoon. I'd like to spend some time with you."

How good it was to hear those words. Never had I felt so confident within myself; how fortunate I was that someone as special as Ralf had shown an interest in me. It would be difficult to arrange to see him, but I found myself agreeing to the idea. We planned to meet when I finished work that afternoon.

How the minutes dragged that day. It was usual for me to buy our evening meal of fish from the harbour on a Saturday afternoon. Father would not expect me to be walking home with him. I suggested I might take a look at the market stalls before going home. My family had no reason to doubt my word, making me feel all the more guilty, but the desire to spend time with Ralf was stronger than any shame.

I adjusted my hair clip, brushed the threads of material from my dress and applied a little scent. With a knot in my stomach and my heart racing, I left the shop to meet Ralf. What a relief to find him waiting for me – I feared he might have had a change of heart.

I suggested we walk to the harbour and he thought it to be an excellent idea. The company was more important than the location, he told me. We walked past the church towards the natural harbour and sandy beach. I told Ralf a little of our local history and he showed an interest.

"How unfortunate for the people of New Romney that they were left without a river or a deep harbour. If the town had remained a thriving port then it would have been very different from the small, quiet town we see today," Ralf commented as he considered my account of the damage done to New Romney by the great storms of the thirteenth century.

"I imagine the town would be like Rye; have you been there?"

"Yes, I have and I believe you are right."

"We have just been to the wedding of my cousin who lives there." How fortunate that I had something of interest to share with Ralf.

Fishing boats lingered just off shore, waiting for the tide which was almost high enough to enable them to beach on the stones. The families of the fishermen gathered to help them either sell the fish to local people or to pack them up to be sent by cart to the towns. There was nothing to do but wait until the tide was ready and I was grateful to be given the excuse to spend more time with Ralf.

"Shall we sit and watch the sea come in? It's relaxing to watch the movement of the water," Ralf said, and took my hand to guide me to a clean area of pebbles.

It was a strange feeling to have Ralf's hand wrapped round mine; a small gesture but it seemed significant for those few seconds, as he helped me walk over a shingle ridge. Then we sat, a little way from the other people, and watched them prepare for the catch to be brought in. We talked about nothing important, mainly his family business: the cloth they made and the places he travelled to, in order to make sales.

"The fish is ready for sale now," I said, reluctant to walk towards the fishermen's stalls. "We need to eat tonight."

"Of course you must and I thank you for spending this time with me. I realise that you have recently lost your betrothed and we must be discreet, but are you able to meet with me tomorrow?" I was so pleased to hear Ralf's words and my heart soared then sank as I realised that it was impossible.

"I really cannot see how… my parents...."

"Oh, don't say that, there must be a way. I promise I can be discreet; I would never harm your good name" He smiled and looked directly into my eyes. I gazed back and was determined to think of a way to make it possible.

"You are kind to think of my feelings. I know my parents would be concerned if I was meeting someone unknown to them," I pondered over what to do. Then I turned to him with a smile and said with resolution, "Aye, I would love to meet you tomorrow. I shall say that I am going to visit my friend, Anna. I will have the whole day."

"It sounds ideal. I could arrange for you to hire a horse from the inn where I am staying. Let us get away from here for the day – shall we go to Hythe?" Ralf's suggestion made my heart leap at the thought of being free from the usual routines and with him all day.

"That would be lovely, but it's all of ten miles away."

"That's no distance to me. Of course we can't meet in the town, but perhaps on the road towards

Dymchurch?"

"I'll wait by the road that leads to the village of St Mary in the Marsh; you'll not find it hard to find." My heart pounded with anticipation. "Does ten o'clock suit you?"

The arrangement was finalised. Ralf thanked me again for sparing the time to be with him that afternoon. There was no need, I would have gladly spent any free time with him. We separated once we reached the churchyard and walked separately to the high street so as not to cause gossip.

I could hardly believe that I could be so easily tempted to deceive my parents and make plans to meet a man who was unknown to them. How I had judged others for flirtatious behaviour; yet here I was behaving in this manner at the first possibility.

Of course, I did feel guilty as I told my parents of my plans to see Anna the next day. Standing before them, I told lies as I had never done before, my awakened heart beating quickly with excitement. I vowed to return in time for the evening church service. Would I be praying for forgiveness or planning another meeting?

It was a relief to find that the weather was fair the next day. I opened the back door and breathed in the fresh spring air. There was so much for me to look forward to. I was the first to rise that morning and was soon busy, lighting the fire to heat both our hot water and the porridge.

Father was not far behind me; there were boots to polish before church and water to draw from the well.

"When do you leave, Jess?"

"I shall check if Mother needs any help and tidy the kitchen after breakfast; then I must hurry if I am to be there and back before church this evening. I expect the horse to be ready and waiting for me when I reach New Romney."

"Give Anna our best wishes and take care on the roads."

I wanted to wear my best dress, the one made of the soft green cloth Ralf had recommended. It was hardly practical for a long horse ride. Instead I chose another dress and spent more time than usual on my hair, using some pretty clips and ribbons. Then I changed my mind and decided that I must look my best so as not to disappoint Ralf. I quickly changed into my favourite dress, hoping that my cloak would protect it from any dirt on the road.

I walked to the town and was relieved to find Ralf waiting for me. He held two horses, one wearing a saddle suitable for a woman. With his usual good manners, he helped me mount and assured me that the horse was known to be of a calm nature. We set off in the direction of Hythe.

I am very fond of my home and immediate surroundings but I felt more comfortable the further we travelled. If someone had seen us together I could have given no explanation as to why I was riding towards Hythe with a male companion. It was awkward to make conversation whilst on horseback and I preferred it that way. The shame of deceiving my parents lay heavy on me.

"Shall we eat first? I expect you are weary after the journey," Ralf asked as we neared Hythe.

"I'd welcome a break; I'm not a competent rider."

"I ride this beast most days; he is a fine horse." Ralf patted the animal's neck with pride.

"I agree." I looked admiringly at both horse and rider.

We were entering the town now and I looked up to

the church on the hillside, a cluster of houses around it. The High Street was quiet, apart from people returning home after the morning church service. Ralf seemed to know the town well and led the way.

"I know of a place that serves a tasty meal. The landlord and his wife are decent people and will be happy to stable the horses." Ralf took control and I was happy to follow his decisions.

A boy came running up as we entered the stable yard.

"Stable the horses whilst we eat, boy. They are in need of a drink and some fresh hay. I'll settle up with the landlord." Ralf motioned for me to dismount and passed both sets of reins to the stable-hand.

The inn seemed to be a respectable establishment. It had tubs of spring flowers at the entrance and fresh sawdust on the floor. I was conscious of the customers looking at us as we entered the main bar, then we were greeted by the landlord.

"Good morning. Ah, Mr... Mr Radcliffe, we've not seen you for some time." He smiled at us, a stout balding man with a ruddy complexion.

"Inviting as your inn may be, I am not tempted to travel so far during the winter. However, the spring has come and I have business in the area again. My friend and I would like a meal in your parlour."

"Certainly, we have a fresh meat pie. Delicious."

"That will do nicely and bring us some wine." Ralf made the decisions for us and I was happy for him to do so. It gave me a comfortable feeling to be so well cared for.

"We'll sit here I think," Ralf gestured to a table as we entered the parlour.

"Have you been here many times before?" I asked

him.

"Several times. The people of Hythe appreciate the fine fabric we make at Radcliffe's Mill. This is the furthest point I travel from Cranbrook and have found it worthwhile to make the journey."

The food came promptly and looked delicious, as promised. We talked as we ate; Ralf had a lot to say about himself and his family. He told me how he had helped to build up the business and how he enjoyed travelling to different areas; it gave him the opportunity to see new places and meet people. His eyes shone with enthusiasm and he was clearly successful in his work. I offered a little information about my own life, but could not expect him to be interested. My daily routines were dull in comparison to his. I listened to him talk, fascinated by his confidence in both himself and the family business, impressed by his success.

Our hunger was satisfied and Ralf suggested we take a walk to the seashore. It was a pleasant afternoon and other people were making the most of the sunshine. We passed an area of common land and paused to watch young people playing handball and another group playing bowls. On reaching the beach, Ralf laid his cloak on a bank of shingle. The tide was approaching and the fishing boats bobbed in the distance.

"Jessica there is something you should know." Ralf spoke in a serious tone and I turned to face him as he seemed to need all my attention. "This will come as a surprise to you. I have told you about my parents and my brother, about my home and my work. There is one more very important part of my life that I have not told you about. I have a child: a baby girl."

"You're married?" A cold numbness spread over me.

"No. My wife died in childbirth; they managed to save the baby. She is ten months old now."

She had died in childbirth. So he was free, perhaps lonely, and the poor baby...

"Your wife died only ten months ago; you must miss her very much."

"She was a good woman. But, Jessica, you must understand, it was a marriage of convenience. My father had been planning it for years; she was an only child and her father owned a rival cloth business. We had the opportunity to merge our assets. She was a suitable wife and I cannot complain, but it was not a love match."

"I understand about such marriages, it's often the way. And now you have a daughter to care for. What's her name?"

"Elizabeth. I'm sure you would love her."

Ralf had said all the things I needed to hear; he was free as to form a new relationship and it was only right that he should. The baby needed a mother to care for her. I was in no position to judge Ralf, to suggest that he should be in mourning. Thoughts of Edmund had been firmly put out of my mind as I had made my plans to meet Ralf and became more and more captivated by him. It was very sad that his wife had died, but I was relieved to hear that it had not been a love match.

"Tell me about Elizabeth," I asked.

As he described her looks, her character and progress, I listened keenly. My heart raced and I was filled with joy for it was clear that Ralf wanted me to be part of his life. I thought of Ralf's words: he had told me that I would love Elizabeth. What could he mean by that? It could only be that I was important enough to meet his daughter one day.

Ralf took my hand and looking straight into my eyes he said: "You are a beautiful, kind-hearted girl and I thank you for your understanding."

I sat mesmerised by his closeness, gazing back into his clear blue eyes. Leaning forward, he kissed me gently on the lips. I had never been kissed like this before; I had never wanted to be kissed before. Our lips parted and his eyes searched my face for some objection, I gave none. We kissed again more passionately and I wanted it never to end. In the distance some men called to each other and we drew slightly apart. Ralf smiled and stood up, offering me his hand to help me to my feet.

"It has been a wonderful day. Thank you for your company." He kissed me lightly on the hand.

"It has," I agreed, lost for any more words.

It was time to return home, back to my life which Ralf was not part of. He was to stay in the area for another week, so at least I would see him again very soon. My horse was returned to the inn and I walked back to Hope. My thoughts were far away, back on the beach in Hythe and my day-dreams full of more perfect days.

It was not until I sat in our damp little church, with my parents either side of me, that I began to feel guilty about lying to them. It would not stop there; over our evening meal they would want to know all the details about my day with Anna – more lies. I knelt and prayed for forgiveness.

Jessica's Story
Chapter Seven

The next time I saw Ralf was the following Wednesday. He called into the shop at the end of the day. Unfortunately, the owner was there and it seemed that there could be no opportunity for us to speak in private. Ralf had different ideas! He had to justify his visit and told us that he was unclear about a recent delivery of cloth. Had we received the full order? Mr Smythe promptly went to the stock room to check.

"Have you had a good week?" I asked.

"Aye, I went to Dymchurch today and made some satisfactory sales." Ralf smiled and continued in a whisper: "I thought of you as I rode along the coast road; I missed your company."

"I had a wonderful day last Sunday," I replied, nervous of being overheard.

"Say you'll meet me on Saturday afternoon, before I go home," Ralf spoke with urgency.

"Well... I"

"It all appears to be correct, Mr Radcliffe," Mr Smythe reported, as he entered the main shop.

"Good news. Thank you for your time, Mr Smythe. Good day to you both." With a smile and a wave he was gone.

I was left wondering if we had an arrangement to

meet on Saturday, unsure of whether it would be possible to see him again. I knew I should introduce Ralf to my parents, of course I should. But what if I were to displease him by making any arrangements?

On my return home that evening, I was surprised to find a sense of calm about the house. I walked straight into the kitchen to find that there had been no meal prepared. Picking up an apron, I started to tie it around my waist and went upstairs to find my mother dozing on her bed.

"Mother?"

"Jess, there you are. How foolish you must think me." She swung her legs off the bed and began to pull herself to her feet. "It's my legs; they ache so, I just couldn't stand for a moment longer. I am sorry about the supper; I've not even brought the vegetables in."

"The supper will be cooking in no time, so don't you worry about that. I'll do it every evening and anything else that is needed if it helps you rest and stay healthy." I walked over to her and kissed her gently on the head, "You need to take more care now, Mother. Perhaps I should arrange for another afternoon away from work?"

"That would help, Jess. I've tried to lift my ankles when possible, they puff up so when I stand at the sink or prepare a meal. Now it's my veins too, I have never had them so bad before. But how can I sit around with my legs up all day?"

"You need some help for a few months. What about Isabel from the farm cottages? She is a pleasant woman and only has her husband to care for. I should have thought of it before. Shall I go to see her tomorrow?"

"I'll have to ask your father," Mother said as she sat back on the bed, as if giving in to need for rest. "If he agrees then please call in to see Isabel after work tomorrow."

"I'm sure Father will agree. Leave it to me to arrange everything." I moved towards the doorway and continued: "Just worry about taking the burden from your legs."

I delegated some chores to James and concentrated on preparing a meal for the four of us. As I worked, I thought of my mother's condition. It was no surprise that she should suffer more during this pregnancy; she was no longer a young woman. How could I have been so selfish as not to have given more thought to her needs? Mother must now be my main concern and, from that moment, I knew I should concentrate more on household chores, ensuring that she rested as much as possible.

I had not forgotten Ralf had wanted to see me on the Saturday afternoon. I longed to be with him but was so ashamed about my neglect of Mother that I resolved to tell him that we could not meet. He was waiting outside the shop for me.

"Jessica, it's lovely to see you." My heart spun when I saw him, as it always did.

"Ralf, how are you?"

"I am well, as always. Selling plenty of cloth and thinking of a pretty girl I would like to spend some time with."

"I am sorry, Ralf. My mother is ill; I am needed at home today. I wish it could be different, but I must go to the farm for dairy produce and straight home to prepare the supper."

"What a shame. Are you sure?"

"Aye, I have neglected her enough recently."

"Well, I must walk with you if it is the only way we

can be together."

"Perhaps just a little way…" I was so disappointed that I could not be with Ralf for any longer. He would be returning home the next day and I knew it would be several months before we met again.

But Ralf had a surprise for me. "I have decided to delay my return home until Monday," he announced. "I was hoping that you would be free to spend Sunday afternoon with me."

"I *wish* I could, but my mother..." I began.

"I altered my arrangements so as to be with you; I thought you would be pleased." His disappointment was clear.

"I would love to... of course I would." If I denied Ralf then his interest in me would wane. I couldn't expect him to understand how much my mother relied on me; my family concerns were nothing to him.

I found myself agreeing to meet Ralf for a walk in the countryside; he suggested we take some food and enjoy a lunch outside. I was soon thinking of missing the morning church service and meeting at this time when it was less likely we would be seen together. I could meet him for a couple of hours and still be able to help Mother as much as needed.

On Sunday morning I rose early in order to complete as many chores as I could. Then I suggested that I take my tapestry and find a peaceful spot where I could sew and watch the lambs in the fields. Mother helped me to prepare lunch and by midmorning I left the cottage, with promises to be back within a few hours to prepare supper before the evening service.

It was a warm, sunny day with a light breeze. The lane leading towards New Romney was lined with blossom-heavy hawthorn bushes. I scurried along, eager to be with Ralf. In the distance the church bells rang and all around the lambs bleated. I left the lane and made my way up a footpath. Once out of sight from the road, I waited for Ralf.

"Jessica, here at last!" Ralf appeared from behind me. He bent down and kissed me lightly.

"You startled me; you were hiding!"

"Just lying in wait for a comely woman." He always knew how to make me feel special.

We followed the footpath which was partly lined with bushes and stunted trees. Our route passed within sight of the farm, but I saw no one in the yard or the fields beside it. Now, there were no more houses and I began to relax. We came to a wide dyke, which we crossed by a footbridge. It was an attractive spot with fresh reeds sprouting on each bank and a pair of swans parading up and down.

"This is as pretty as any place we are likely to find on the Romney Marsh," Ralf commented. "Shall we sit here for a while?"

"It seems to be quite private. Mother packed me some bread, cheese and fruit." I opened the bag to show Ralf. "I couldn't bring too much as they think I am out alone."

"I have some pie; I begged my landlady for it." Ralf produced a large piece of meat pie. "So, we shall eat well and with good company there is little more to wish for."

We spread a rug on the grass and settled down to eat and talk. The day had started with fine weather, but as we relaxed, we noticed the skies to the east rapidly darkening.

It looks as if there is some heavy rain coming our way," I commented at last, loathe to put an end to this wonderful day.

"Perhaps it will miss us; I feel nothing can spoil our time together," Ralf replied, as he lay back on the rug.

Then he turned to face me, propped his head upon his arm, reached out and gently pulled my face towards him. We kissed and I forgot about my fears that someone would see us. I forgot the guilt I felt for deceiving my parents and forgot about the approaching rain. When Ralf kissed me, nothing else was important.

I became aware that the air now had a chill to it and the sun was concealed by dark clouds. It was clearly going to rain heavily at any moment. We were too far from home to attempt to get back in time. Ralf gathered up our belongings and, as the first large drops of rain fell, we ran for the shelter of a group of willow trees. They were barely adequate to protect us from a downpour.

"What is that little hut? Surely it's not large enough to be a cottage?" Ralf pointed to a stone hut in the centre of the next field.

"It's a looker's hut; we need the shelter and it should be empty."

We ran across the field, hand in hand. As we neared the hut, the heavens opened and I could barely see for the rain streaming down my face. I hung back as Ralf opened the door and checked that it was vacant. Then he pulled me inside.

I took off my cloak and hung it over a stool. My hair was soaking wet and I attempted to dry it with my skirt.

"Your dress is wet at the top too… I would feel so guilty if you caught a cold," Ralf murmured as he touched the damp fabric.

His hand strayed to my breasts and stayed there as he looked into my eyes, daring me to oppose him. I knew I should not allow it, but could not find the words to refuse Ralf; I was mesmerised by him. We kissed and still I knew that he should remove his hand but I had no desire to ask him to.

"Oh, Jess." Ralf moved away from me, just a little.

I didn't want the rain to end. This time I moved forward to kiss Ralf. His response was so passionate I felt that my heart would burst. He turned and swiftly threw the picnic rug over the floor. Ralf sat down; still holding my hand he pulled me down beside him. We kissed again and he gently pushed me back on to the rug, pausing for a split second – perhaps to see if I would object. He kissed my neck, then my hair, until I could no longer think clearly. His lips returned to mine. As we kissed, Ralf ran his hands up and down my body then slipped them into my bodice.

A voice inside me screamed out: "He should not be doing this; I should not allow it; this is for when we are married." I ignored it.

Ralf took my hand and guided it down to the bulge beneath his breeches, I explored this unknown territory. Still the voice told me to stop. Yet I relished the attention Ralf gave me, and was overwhelmed with the passions he provoked. As one of his hands moved further down my body the other loosened his breeches, allowing me to explore further. I had no inclination to stop myself from finding out what was to happen next…

Afterwards, we lay on the rug, Ralf gently stroking my hair and telling me he loved me. I had never imagined such passions could exist, as I was totally ignorant of those relations between a man and woman. He loved me, it was all that mattered and I felt no repentance.

The rain stopped as quickly as it came, the grey clouds continuing on their way. We had no excuse to linger any more in the looker's hut and opened the door to find the countryside was glistening.

"No regrets?" Ralf asked gently as we left the hut.

"Only that we are to part now; when shall I see you again?"

"I cannot be parted from you for long; I'll do my best...."

"We have the May Day celebrations soon. It would be wonderful if you were able to be here."

"I promise to be there!"

"Oh, but what of your daughter? I'm sorry, I have been selfish and you will want to be with her."

"No, not at all, she is young and better in the care of her aunt. She needs a woman's loving care. I will be there."

We kissed before separating, with regrets we were to be parted and promises it would not be for long.

"I have neglected your future, Jessica." I was surprised to hear my father make the sudden announcement.

Mother and I were busy sewing some tiny clothes for the new baby. It had been two weeks since I last saw Ralf, but I felt comfortable in the knowledge he would return soon. My mother had the extra help in the home that she needed and seemed to be in good health. I was very content with my life.

"Oh, Father. I am happy and we are all keeping well. You could not neglect me," I replied.

"You are seventeen years old. If life had been different then you would have been married to Edmund. Any man would be proud to call you his wife, as we are proud to call you our daughter. Most women of your age are planning marriage and it is time I considered your future." My father was right, and I waited to hear whether he had made arrangements for another marriage.

"Clement, have you someone in mind?" my mother asked, all thoughts of sewing driven from her mind.

"Not yet, perhaps Thomas. Or even Nathan; I believe he may have matured a little." My father frowned slightly as he considered the options.

"Father, I must tell you..." I burst out. Then I stopped – how should I tell him? I continued, with hesitance, "Thank you for your concern, Father. There is something I should tell you: do not think that I don't value your choice, but I have met someone."

"Jess?" both parents replied in unison.

"His name is Ralf. He comes to New Romney to sell the cloth produced by his family's business. He has been into the drapery many times and shown an interest in spending time with me. I have met him in the town, at the harbour and I once showed him the church he... he was interested in the history." I was nervous, wondering what their response would be.

"I have no need to ask if you have behaved correctly with this man." My father spoke solemnly and I felt so guilty at his words. "Do you see your future being with Ralf?"

"I hope so, Father." I told them a little about Ralf, mainly about his home and the successful trade he was involved in. "I've asked him to come to our May Day celebrations; you could meet him then?"

"That sounds ideal and I can judge his character for myself."

Jessica's Story
Chapter Eight

The long-awaited May Day arrived and I was filled with suppressed excitement. I was to see Ralf again and could hardly wait a moment longer. Nerves fluttered around my stomach. Would my parents like and approve of him? Surely they would be pleased that a man such as Ralf had shown an interest in their daughter?

The family prepared to walk to New Romney. We dressed in our best outfits and took coins we had saved, in order to treat ourselves to food and possibly buy fancy goods from a pedlar. As we were about to leave my father approached me and handed me a shawl of fine lace.

"This is a special day for you; the chance to introduce Ralf to your family. We thought you might like this for May Day."

"Thank you Father, it's beautiful," I held up the shawl to admire it. "I do want to look my best today."

"You know better than to ask where it came from."

We walked towards New Romney and the road became busier as other people left their rural homes for a welcome break to the usual routine. Children skipped ahead of parents and sang popular rhymes. Everyone wore their best outfits; the women had flowers in their hair and wore ribbons, lace and jewellery.

Before we reached the town, the tunes played by the fiddlers could be heard. They were joined by the occasional cheer or shout, carried to us on the breeze. Gradually the sounds of music and voices became less disjointed and we turned the corner to view the celebrations.

Our eyes were drawn to the tall maypole, standing almost as high as a house. Ribbons hung from the pole and the ground around it was strewn with straw. Boughs of blossom surrounded the dancing area which would soon be the centre of all the activities. Young girls sat around the maypole, hoping to be among the first to dance.

Of equal importance were the spits upon which meat was roasting. Small boys earned themselves a tasty meal by sparing some time to turn it. It was a day for feasting: bakers brought mutton pies straight from the ovens to sell whilst they were still hot; fishermen sold shellfish from barrows.

We paused to savour the scene; it was one of the highlights of the year for many people. A time to dance and feast, to forget our problems for the day and be merry. The fiddler struck up a popular tune and was soon joined by the drum, trumpet and hautboy. I found myself tapping my foot in time to the music; it was an infectious melody. Young people were soon dancing vigorously around the maypole. They jostled each other and tried to avoid their feet being stamped upon, or their ribbon becoming twisted into knots. Whatever the dancers lacked in style or grace, they gained in enthusiasm!

My gaze moved amongst the groups of people, to the queues at food stalls and the solitary onlookers. Was he here yet? I couldn't see his slim figure and dark hair. It really was too early to expect Ralf yet, but I was impelled to search for him.

"What a merry tune. Jessica, will you join me for a dance?" Nathan approached with Thomas and Ellen.

"Oh... I... have you just arrived?"

I wasn't sure whether to dance yet, or should I wait for Ralf? He could be another hour or more, so it was foolish not to enjoy the celebrations. Yet, what if he were to arrive and see me dancing with Nathan? What if Ralf were to think that my affections were fickle?

"We were eager to get here as soon as we could," Nathan replied. "James, I know that you'll dance with us around the maypole. Help me persuade the girls to join in the fun."

"Say you will Jessica," James pulled at my hand.

"You don't need to beg me, let's go over so as to be ready when they start the next tune." I handed my shawl to my mother, the dancing had little order to it and I didn't want the lace to be damaged.

"I'm sure to trip and Nathan leaps around so much that he is a danger to the other dancers!" Ellen giggled as we walked towards the maypole.

"I'll have you know I'm a good dancer," Nathan replied with a laugh. "Now hurry up; they are starting again. James, take that ribbon."

"Ellen, Jessica, are you ready?" Thomas was more considerate than his brother and gave us both a ribbon. "Be careful to avoid Nathan, you know how careless he is!"

The musicians launched into a well-known tune and we danced one way, then the other, exchanging places with each other and trying to keep a secure hold on the ribbons. Most people had some experience of the dances, but were not well practised.

Dancers made mistakes and others followed, people called out directions to each other, and we happily muddled through. The music ended abruptly and we fell to the ground for a rest on the straw.

People gathered to dance as the next tune started and we moved away, so as to give them some space. James saw a boy he knew, and left us to be with someone nearer his own age; I saw them watching a juggler, fascinated by his skill. Ellen suggested we look at what the pedlars had to sell. Thomas and Nathan had no interest in that; Nathan preferred to watch the dancing while Thomas met up with other young farmers.

The pedlars were often poor men with no fixed home. They travelled between the towns and villages, trying to sell jewellery and trinkets. The best opportunity for them to make money was on the day of a fair or annual celebration. Even the poorest people saved up a little money to treat themselves to something special.

One pedlar was a slight man, with a cheery face and a gaudy waistcoat over travel-stained clothes. He had hired a table on which he displayed the products he wished to sell. As we came near, he called out and waved his hands towards the goods.

"Now, here are young ladies who will be interested in some coloured ribbon or pretty glass beads. Come and see what takes your fancy."

We stepped closer to the table and smiled shyly at the man. Ellen picked up some ribbons and compared the colours.

"Ah, a nice length of ribbon will look lovely in your curly hair." Then he turned to me and pointed at some hair clips. "And what about you? I bet you've got a young man who you want to make yourself pretty for. I know what young ladies like; how about one of those hair clips?"

Ellen giggled at his comments. I found his attitude to be overly familiar and felt uncomfortable. I avoided his gaze and concentrated on the brooches and pendants. Finally, I selected a small enamelled pendant, hanging from a ribbon. Ellen chose some ribbon and a hair clip.

"Thank you, young ladies. Enjoy your day; May Day comes only once a year!" He then turned to concentrate on his new customers and I vowed to avoid his stall for the rest of the day.

Ellen and I wandered around, stopping to watch the dancers or to speak to an acquaintance. I found it difficult to concentrate on anything, for I knew it could not be long now before Ralf arrived. It was important that I did not miss a minute of the time available with him. I looked one way and another, searching for that first glimpse of him.

The mutton pies, straight from the baker's oven, smelt very tempting. A young lad carried a tray of them and was stopped as he walked, selling his goods whilst they were steaming hot. Ellen bought one, but I decided that I would prefer to wait for Ralf. There would be more later.

An hour passed and it was early afternoon. I sat with my parents and listened to the fiddlers' merry tunes.

"Have you not eaten yet?" Mother asked me. She looked anxious.

"I was waiting for Ralf."

"He has a long way to come; don't starve yourself, Jess. Treat yourself to one of those pies or some roast meat from the spit."

The food smells were mouth-watering; there was

no harm in eating before Ralf came and he wouldn't expect me to wait. Mother was right, he could be delayed on the road. I decided to have some bread and meat.

Another hour passed. Mother had bought me some ballad sheets, which were often sold on fair days. It was our opportunity to catch up on the new songs becoming fashionable in London and the larger towns. Within a few weeks, the songs would become popular and local people singing along to the words or learning to play the tunes. I glanced at the words but remembered none of them. My thoughts were all with Ralf.

"Jess, come and watch the Morris dancers. You always enjoy them," Mother said, smiling her encouragement.

"No, I'll stay here." I had no inclination to get up and try to enjoy the rest of the afternoon. It was getting late and I was beginning to wonder if Ralf would come at all. This day had been so important to me but now it was tarnished with disappointment and humiliation.

"It's mid-afternoon; do you think that we'll see Ralf today?" Mother asked gently. "It is such a long journey and we cannot know if he was unable to travel. Perhaps his family needed him."

"I know, he couldn't say... couldn't let me know. There will be a reason." It didn't take away the pain in my heart though; how foolish of me.

"Jess, I am sure Ralf is a good man," Mother began with hesitation. "Your father and I only want you to be happy; would it not be more suitable for you to settle for a local man? Someone whom you have known all your life and whose family we know."

"You speak too soon, Mother. Ralf may not be here yet, but perhaps next week..."

As the afternoon progressed, dancers became less enthusiastic and musicians paused more frequently for breaks. The remainder of the food would soon be sold off cheaply. I sat watching the activities, but not really seeing them.

All I could see was a picture of Ralf's face; all I could hear was his voice. I remembered the times we had been alone together and how special they had been. I must believe he would come soon, for the alternative was unbearable.

We started to walk home, James talking with enthusiasm about the day. My father listened to him and agreed it had been a great celebration. Mother walked slowly, she was tired as was to be expected in the seventh month of her pregnancy. She looked at me with a sympathy I did not want to see.

Four weeks after the May Day celebrations, we had another excuse for merrymaking. On Whitsun it was traditional for potent ale to be sold in order to raise funds for the parish church. Our small village had decreased in residents over the past few years, so, the parish had become poorer and the church was in disrepair. The parson needed all the money he could raise in order to keep All Saints safe and dry.

I had no enthusiasm for another party, but it would be noticed if I didn't make the effort to join in. There had been no visit from Ralf in the weeks since May Day and I found myself frequently dwelling on his absence and wondering what had become of him. There was a reasonable explanation; I prayed for it.

The family dressed in their good clothes. My mother was so heavily pregnant that she now walked no further than the farm or the church. She leant on my father's arm as we crossed the road and walked along the bumpy track to the church. The bells rang out joyfully. Our neighbours gathered for the morning service. For the next half an hour we sang, listened to the sermon and prayed.

"Now go in peace to love and serve the Lord," our parson concluded the service. "Before we all leave today, I would like to thank you for your generous donations of food and especially the roast lamb kindly prepared by the women at the farm – there is plenty for all on the tables outside. Let us be grateful for all we have and enjoy the Whitsun celebrations;. John has brought his pipe and my niece, Sara, has her fiddle, so we can all delight in some music."

The next hour followed the familiar pattern. The men drank ale, the elderly women gossiped and the younger women watched over their families. The children of James' age and younger had fun playing games. The younger children trailed after the older children, eager to be included. The young adults, which included only myself and the family from the farm, danced, ate and played with the children. We made a small gathering, but loyally supported our church.

Mother was sitting on a bench that someone had kindly provided for her. She looked a little restless.

"Are you feeling unwell, Mother? Can I get you anything?" I asked with concern.

"It's just a little indigestion; I should know not to eat too much." Mother smiled apologetically, "Would you mind fetching my tonic? You'll find it on my sewing table."

"Of course." I was pleased for the excuse to have a few minutes to myself.

I walked back to our cottage and soon found the bottle of tonic amongst the tiny garments Mother had been sewing and the sheets that needed hemming. I picked one up and admired the detail. I wondered what it would be like to have a baby in the house again. James was eleven years old; eleven years since our mother had last given birth. She need not burden herself with worry about the housework or cooking now; we were fortunate to have Isabel to help us and I was lucky to be able to work a half-day on wash day. I hurried out of the house, back to my family.

"Jessica... Jessica." I heard a man's voice call out. Who could it be? Probably Nathan, playing his silly games. I looked up and down the road.

Someone was standing by the entrance to the farm. I looked again; it couldn't be, but it was – Ralf! There was no mistake, he was waving at me. I hurried towards him.

"Ralf, you came at last."

"Jessica, how good to see you. Say that you'll spend some time with me."

"Of course. We are having a small Whitsun celebration. My family will be so pleased to meet you."

"It's been so long, Jess. Let us be alone together."

"Oh, I..."

"I'd love to meet your family, of course I would. But, then we shall never be alone and we can meet so infrequently."

If Ralf wanted to be alone with me then I could not refuse him. How fortunate I was to have his attention.

"You are right of course. They would be so pleased to meet you, but we'd never have a minute to ourselves. I must take this tonic to my mother and I will be back within minutes."

"I'll wait here."

I made my excuses to Mother. I had a headache

and needed to rest for a while. Meat pies were being sold and I decided to buy a couple as Ralf may be hungry. Soon I was back with him.

"We need to get further away from everyone. We can't stay here." I couldn't relax until we were away from prying eyes.

"How about that little hut? It was peaceful there." Ralf smiled and took my hand to lead me towards the footpath.

I blushed at the memories. How wrong of me to go there again with him. "Ralf... I waited for you on May Day."

"May Day?"

"I was expecting you; I know there must have been a reason. Could you not leave your family?"

We were away from the road now and had walked past the farm buildings. There was no one to be seen. Ralf pulled me towards him and kissed me with passion. My doubts faded, he had clearly not lost interest.

"I am sorry, dearest," he looked at me tenderly. "It was Elizabeth; she had a fever. How could I leave her?"

"Is she well now?" I asked. An infant's life was fragile.

"She is perfectly well. It may have been that she was teething, but how can you tell? Thankfully, she is as healthy as ever." Ralf smiled at me, then added: "And for today we concentrate on ourselves!"

As we followed the footpath, we spoke about our lives since our last meeting. There was little for me to tell as mine was dull in comparison with his. I told him a little about our May Day celebrations, but did not want to bore him with my news. Ralf spoke about the places he had visited and the continued success of his family business. Again I thought about how lucky I was that he had any interest in me, for his days were filled with his rewarding work and experiences unknown to me.

    The track soon led us to the field with the looker's hut in it. The hut in which we had sheltered from the rain. The hut in which I had abandoned my morals and behaved in a way most unlike myself. Ralf looked towards it, then turned to me and smiled. He took my hand and gently guided me in the direction of the hut and I gave no objections.

James was sitting on the front door step as I approached the cottage. He jumped up and ran towards me. "Jess, where have you been? It's Mother, her pains have started. She is asking for you."

Jessica's Story
Chapter Nine

"It's too early," I said, partly to myself, as I rushed into the house and upstairs to my mother.

My father was outside the bedroom. He sat with his head in his hands and looked up to see me. "The midwife is with your mother. Her pains started a couple of hours ago; they've lessened a little and we are hoping that the baby will choose to wait for a few more weeks. She'll want to see you, Jess."

Mother was raised by cushions on the bed in the darkened room. She looked exhausted, but managed to smile as I entered the room.

"We've had a scare. I started having pains, but they're not so frequent now. I pray the baby will wait a little longer." She paused to take the weak wine offered by the midwife. "It's too early for it to come."

"Is this normal?" I asked the midwife.

"Your mother had a slight fall earlier, which has brought on early labour. It seems it has stopped, but the baby could still come early. She must rest now as much as possible," the midwife told me. She was an experienced woman and we trusted her opinion.

"You had a fall, Mother? I didn't realise, I should have been with you." I felt so guilty, for yet again I had been selfish and irresponsible.

"I'm much better now, Jessica. Please let your

father and James know that all is well. The pains have eased."

I did as she asked and then began to prepare supper. The midwife left to return home, with promises to check on Mother in the morning. None of us could concentrate on anything that evening as we dwelt on Mother's condition. I sat with her, talking and sewing.

The following day, I arranged to have a half-day at work. I couldn't focus on anything and went from one task to another with no order to my work. Mr and Mrs Smythe were sympathetic, understanding my concern for Mother's health. I had seen Ralf earlier that morning when he had come into the shop. Mr Smythe had dealt with the order for cloth and we had been unable to talk. I was unsure of whether I would be able to see him again during this visit as he was to leave for Cranbrook that afternoon.

I took the decision to ask Mr Smythe if I could go to the apothecary to buy a tonic for Mother. Feeling guilty for the deception, I walked along the High Street, scanning the area for a sign of my love. Just in time, I saw him leaving the inn.

"Jessica, there is no time for me to stop now; I should be on the road home." Ralf was already on horseback, and about to start his journey.

"I just came to say 'goodbye', for it may be months before we meet again."

"It will be weeks, I promise you! I'll travel this way again within the month and then I hope we are able to spend more time together."

"I hope so too, Ralf. It's so difficult."

"That is true. Jessica, when I return we shall make plans for the future… our future."

"Ralf…"

"Goodbye for now, I'll be thinking of you." From his

horse, he looked down at me and said: "Until next time..."

"Goodbye, Ralf."

His words rang in my ears as I walked along the street to the apothecary. Make plans for the future... He, Ralf, had *really* said those words: "*We shall make plans for the future... our future.*"

It was on the Saturday night, just six days after the false alarm, that my mother went into labour – still four weeks before the baby was due. In the morning, James borrowed a pony from the farm and rode to fetch the midwife. All day I kept a pan of hot water and clean towels ready for the birth. The pains continued to tire Mother, yet they came no closer. As afternoon turned into evening, there was still no sign of the baby. The midwife was concerned and gave various remedies to try to induce a speedier delivery.

It was not until the early hours of the next morning that the baby arrived. He gave no welcoming cry to the world; the fight had been too great for his tiny, feeble body. He was laid in a wooden box to await a blessing from the parson later that morning. The shock was no less, despite this being a common occurrence. Mother was too exhausted to show much emotion. She was weakened due to loss of blood and sunk low by the death of her child.

Father arranged for me to have time away from work to care for Mother. I tried to encourage her to eat but she remained lethargic, with no appetite. I busied myself with the housework, cooking and trying various herbal remedies in an attempt to lift her spirits. Within two days of the birth, my mother began to suffer from a fever. I washed her down with cool water; it gave her no relief. Within another day she was barely conscious. We called for the priest to pray for her soul and by Thursday she joined her baby in heaven.

James was very tearful; Father and I were numb with shock and grief. There was no time to wallow in our time of mourning; the household chores were never ending and there was a funeral to arrange. Mother and baby, whom we named Edward, were together beside the graves of my other brother and sister. Many local people came to pay their last respects. My mother was a kind, gentle woman who had been well-loved.

My responsibilities in the home increased after the death, although twice a week Isabel continued to help with cleaning the house and preparing vegetables for our supper. The greatest chore was the washing of our clothes, although there was less to wash, dry and press now. There was no time to rest after work; I had to prepare a meal using the meat or fish I bought during my lunch break.

My father arranged for James to work on the farm in the afternoon, under the guidance of Thomas. It was good for James to keep himself busy and distracted from dwelling on our mother's death. For Father and myself, it was a relief to know James was occupied in a useful way.

The burden of housework began to take its toll on my own health. Although grateful to Isabel, I felt that I had to be responsible for most aspects of caring for the home and family. With Mother gone, I had no close female friend or relative in my life. Headaches began to plague me and I felt so tired from the moment I rose in the morning until bedtime. There was little time for me to rest. It was a lonely time for me.

"You look weary, Jess; let Isabel take on more of

the chores in the home," my father said.

"No, Father, it's my duty. Perhaps a little tonic will lift my spirits?"

"You must go to the apothecary. Promise me you will."

I did as he asked and was given a bottle of liquid tonic. I also bought some ginger to help ease the sickness which came with the early morning headaches. Gradually I began to feel a little better. The warm summer sun was soothing and I began to accept the death of my mother.

I gave little thought to Ralf during this time. It had been about a month since Whitsun and although he had promised me he would be travelling to Romney Marsh in the near future, it was likely that he had business in other areas and would not come to New Romney for another month at least. If he had appeared, I couldn't have spared any time for him. I realised, with a sinking heart, that the death of my mother had brought with it the end of any dreams I had of being with Ralf. It would be selfish of me to leave my father and James now. My love's home in Cranbrook was too far away. He had not mentioned marriage but had hinted at it and I was sure that the next time he visited he would want to make definite plans for our future. I knew I would have to tell him we could not be together. The thought of losing him weighed heavy on me and the headaches returned.

It was not until the beginning of July it slowly dawned on me that there could be another reason for my recent ill health. My stomach was feeling bloated and, as I expected my monthly show of blood to come, I tried to remember when my last one was. I could not remember having one since... since before Lizzie's wedding. Could my moment of intimacy with Ralf have led to pregnancy? I was unsure, but it seemed to be likely. The full horror of my situation suddenly hit me and slumped on my bed, my head pounding.

There was no one for me to confide in. I would have to wait to see if any other symptoms developed. By the middle of July I felt much better, had more energy, my skin glowed and my hair shone. If it were not for the thickening around my stomach and waist I could have believed all was well. There was no longer any doubt I was expecting Ralf's baby.

It is hard to describe how I felt: mortified knowing the shame I would bring upon our family; concerned about my father's response; guilty that my mother went to her grave believing that she had a chaste and honourable daughter; ashamed of my sins. I went to the church daily to pray for guidance and forgiveness.

At the same time, I could not help feeling relieved I had been given the reason I needed to enable me to be with Ralf. If he and I were meant to be together then what could be more natural than to have a baby together? We should have waited until we were married, but I was sure Ralf would know how to deal with the situation.

When my love did eventually travel to New Romney again, it was the end of July and my stomach had a very gentle swell. I wondered if he would notice any difference in me. When he came into the shop, I was just about to leave for my lunch break.

"Will you walk to the harbour with me?" I asked.

"Are you not concerned we might be seen together?" Ralf laughed in surprise.

"It doesn't matter." It was too late for that; we needed to talk.

I was quiet as we walked to the shingle bank where the fishermen sold their latest catch. How would

Ralf react to the news? I had convinced myself that he would be happy to marry me and all would be well, but now I was not too sure.

"Ralf, there is something I have to tell you." The words came out in a rush; there was no point in delaying the news. "I am expecting a baby."

"Jessica, how?" I had never seen him stuck for words.

"It is a shock, I know. There is no doubt about it."

"It certainly is a shock. You are sure, you say?"

"I am sure," I confirmed.

"When is it due?" Now his words came in a rush. "Have you told your family?"

"Perhaps at the end of the year?" I was unsure, having been unable to discuss my condition with anyone. "I've told no one. My mother is dead and I thought it best to wait for you."

"Your mother died?"

I told Ralf of the recent events in our family. A lot had happened since I last saw him at Whitsun. I think he was only half listening; no doubt his thoughts were on the child I was expecting – his child.

"Jessica, you have had a dreadful time but don't worry. Everything will be fine now; I shall look after you." Ralf said the words I needed to hear.

"It will be difficult to leave my family, but they'll manage. Perhaps we'll have a son; you'd like that." My heart was light and the future seemed idyllic. "I shall be able to look after your daughter too; do you think she'll like to have a baby brother?"

"Aye, I'm sure Elizabeth would love a baby brother," Ralf smiled. "Imagine that – a son!"

"What of your family?" I reddened as I thought of my thickening waist. "It's too late to marry and pretend the baby is premature."

"These things happen in all families. Now, let me think about what's to be done."

I gave Ralf some time to consider the news, while I bought the fish for our evening meal. He seemed to be deep in thought. I joined him again and we walked back towards the town, speaking quietly.

"You must come to see my family, Ralf. If we are to be together then Father will need to meet you. Should we tell him about the baby, or wait?"

"No, it will cause him great worry at this time when he has just lost his wife and baby. I have been thinking and it is best if I return home tomorrow and tell my family about you. When I return, we can tell your father. Then we can make arrangements." Ralf had made the decision; I could trust him to know the best way to do things.

"Do your family know of me?"

"I know they'll love you, as I do."

"There's not much time; I'll begin to show soon."

"Don't worry, I'll return within a week or two. It will be no longer, I promise. We must part now and I'll make haste for Cranbrook with the good news." He flashed a smile and continued: "It will not be long and I'll be returning for you, my love."

"I'll be waiting for you Ralf and praying for a healthy son, for I know that's what you'll want."

I watched him walk down the street, but this time I did not mind him leaving. I knew that Ralf was going to arrange our future. He would return soon and once we were married it would not matter too much that the baby had been conceived earlier than it should have been. My only regrets were that I would be leaving my home and family, but the sacrifice was worth it to be with a man such as Ralf.

Anna's Story
Part Two
Chapter One

The stench filled my nostrils, vomit rose in my throat and I forced myself to keep it down, as I picked my way past tables, stools and upturned tankards. Pulling back the bolts on the door, I flung it open and gulped fresh air. Weak, winter sunshine spilt into the tavern, highlighting the amount of work that was to be done.

I started with the tankards, placing them on a tray and taking them to the kitchen sink for my aunt to wash. Then the candles, separating those that would serve another day and those the chandler may use for remoulding. Reaching down to lift a stool upright, I was ready to vomit again – the rushes on the floor were damp and not with ale, but urine. The fire would have to wait now; there was a floor to be cleaned.

"Oh Anna, you are a saint! It's looking better already." My aunt came from the kitchen, her sleeves rolled up, an enormous apron covering her dress. "And you've changed the reeds."

"I had to."

"I see. We've some lavender to scent the new ones. It won't last but we'll have tried." Aunt Emm knelt and started sweeping out the grate.

"What a night, good for business, but I hope today

is quiet." I stood and surveyed the tavern; it looked respectable again.

"We don't need the likes of them, their money isn't needed here," Aunt Emm spoke sharply.

It wasn't often like that; usually customers enjoyed a quiet drink and the company. They might play a game of draughts, shovel-board or cards. It would get a bit rowdier when they had coins in their pocket or on a Saturday night. But the evening before, a group of young men had been celebrating a new child, the first son for the family. They gambled money, wasting what was needed for food, clothing or fuel. Fooling around, they picked a fight and someone went home with a bruised eye and bloody nose.

"Maybe your Michael will be in for a tankard of ale later." Aunt Emm turned from piling the wood in the fireplace and looked directly at me.

"He's not my Michael," I insisted, and he wasn't.

"He would like to be."

"Maybe he would, but he's not."

"Not Thomas, not the man who hurt you, let you down? No, Michael is a good man, a decent man."

He was a good man and I knew it. I'd seen enough bad ones since I had been at the inn, boozing and gambling. He was one of the hard working, dependable men who came in for a drink and a talk in the early evening. He was a doctor too, well liked and respected in the community. I knew he could offer me a better life than serving in a tavern and clearing up after other people. He was, as I said, a good man, but he was not Thomas.

"It's clean and tidy for now. I'll go out for some fresh milk and meat before we get busy." My apron was exchanged for a warm cloak and a basket was taken from a hook on the wall.

"Take your time; you need some fresh air, so no need to hurry back. And, Anna, if you meet Michael... be kind."

There was still frost underfoot as I walked along the road. Mother and I had become quite settled here in the past three years. The village of Appledore suited us, with a good selection of shops, a fine church and people who accepted us into their community. Aunt Emm was a cheerful woman who appreciated the help we gave in the tavern and had welcomed us into her home. Behind the inn was a hotchpotch of rooms added on when needed, but all in good repair and with a newly thatched roof.

Appledore lay on higher ground at the very edge of Romney Marsh. In one direction the countryside rose, there was less need for drainage and there were woods and hills. In the other direction, looking towards the sea, was the very lowest area of the marsh, known as the Appledore Dowels. It was this area that gave Appledore the reputation of being unhealthy as water lay stagnant in the dykes, tempting the mosquitoes who brought with them a form of malaria known as the Marsh Ague.

Once the shopping was done, I had no need to linger and turned for home. There was always the chance that I might meet Michael and I preferred to avoid him for now. Over the past few months, he had fallen into the pattern of walking home from church with us on a Sunday and had occasionally stopped for lunch. At first he made the excuse of wanting to speak with my mother about the expectant mothers and newborn babies, for he had been supportive in encouraging her to work as a midwife again. To Mother and Aunt Emm, it was obvious that his true interest was in myself. More recently I had admitted, with reluctance, that it seemed to be true. He was always polite and considerate and I found myself agreeing to a walk on Sunday afternoons. Michael spoke, not directly, but hinted of our future together.

On my return, Mother was in the kitchen, shaking sugar over a fruit pie. She placed it on the table with bread, cold meat and pickled vegetables. Looking towards me she said: "Your Aunt Emm will eat lunch at the bar, give us a chance to have a talk."

"Shall I take it in for her?"

"If you would." Swiftly, she produced a wooden plate and placed a selection of food on it. "There you are, and tell her there's a fruit pie to follow."

Back in the kitchen, the air was thick with smoke from the fire. The lime-washed walls were grey, but the window had been cleaned that morning and the dresser, with all the dishes and pans on it, was dust free. The rugs were hanging in the yard, the dirt having been beaten out of them. A jug with branches of winter berries and evergreen leaves was placed on the table.

"It's time to think seriously about your future, Anna." The bread was in her hand, but Mother wanted to talk before she ate. "Nineteen years old. You should be married with little ones of your own."

"I had thought I would be."

"That was three years ago now. Do you think Thomas Farley is worth waiting for?"

"I'm not waiting for him, I just..." I wasn't waiting for him, really I wasn't. I knew better than that.

"He'll marry a farmer's daughter, no doubt. The farm needs an heir."

"Eliza says he never married." I broke the bread into small pieces and toyed with them on my plate.

"There's many a decent man who would be proud

to call you his wife, Anna. I see them watching you, admiring your pretty fair hair falling down your back, your trim figure and nice manners."

"I don't notice them."

"You give them no encouragement." Then, reaching out for my arm, eyes soft but probing, she tried once more. "Please Anna, think about Michael. You know how he adores you. It's time to think to the future, time to make the most of this opportunity."

"I'll think about it; I really will. I promise."

Satisfied, Mother settled down to enjoy the food, her eyes frequently flitting to my face, hoping to read my thoughts.

The conversation was fresh in my mind when Michael and his brother came in for a drink early that afternoon. They often looked towards me; I stood tall and returned the smiles. Encouraged, Michael came to refill their tankards.

"The weather looks to be fair tomorrow. Would you care for a walk in the afternoon?" He stood before me with an arm on the bar, not tall but of average height. His face was pleasant and friendly, his hair brown with neat waves. "I'd like your company."

"That would be lovely." My bright smile was forced.

It was quiet that afternoon. I busied myself tidying the games of backgammon and draughts and was considering cleaning the windows when the door opened. The fireplace and chimney stood in the centre of the room obscuring my view of the new arrival. Aunt Emm was at the bar waiting to serve.

"A tankard of ale, please." His voice was deep, familiar, but from the past.

"Certainly. You've not been in here before, just passing through?" Aunt Emm was always inquisitive.

"I have business in the area." Again, that voice: friendly, confident, taking me back...

"A farmer, are you?"

"That's right. I have land not far from New Romney."

"New Romney?" I could hear the uncertainty in Emm's voice, the words were sharp. "New Romney, you say?"

I froze where I stood, my throat constricted, then slowly the blush rose from my neck to my cheeks. I turned, wanting it to be him... it must be him... but dreading the return of all my pain. I looked up and his eyes were on me, his expression serious, as if waiting for my reaction. He took a step forwards, stooping to avoid a beam. In the dimly lit bar, his face was clearer now; perhaps he had aged slightly and his red-brown hair was a little longer. His brown eyes looked rather sad and his smile was hesitant.

"I hope I'm welcome here."

"I...I don't know." The words were stiff; I was cold and stiff with apprehension. I turned to the fire and added another log. Reaching forward, I warmed my hands.

"Can we talk?"

"Of course," I replied.

Looking past him, I noticed that my mother was standing, open mouthed, beside my aunt. I stepped past Thomas, so close that our clothes touched and I felt my heart contract. I could smell those familiar scents of the farm, the animals and their feed. A picture flashed into my head of the large farmhouse kitchen: herbs hanging in bunches, dishes of fruit, jars of preserves. Perhaps a pig roasting on a spit above a fire.

"Mistress Smith, good to see you." He spoke

clearly, not knowing how she would react.

"Thomas," Mother looked directly at him. "It's been a long time."

"It has, too long, I know."

"You can speak in the kitchen."

I led the way through a storeroom and into the dark, stuffy room. Opening the door which led to the yard, I let in some fresh air. The shaft of light was full of dancing dust. He sat in silence, but I could feel his eyes on me as I took hot water and made us both a drink of camomile, then placed plates and fruit pie on the table. I sat opposite Thomas; it was time to talk.

"I missed you, Anna. I should have come before." His voice was low, his eyes looking straight into mine, arms on the table. He leant forward slightly.

"Why would you come? There is no future for us, you made that clear."

"I want that to change; I treated you badly. If there is nothing to keep you here, then I beg of you to come home, back to me."

"Return to Hope, to be shunned by people I knew, to cause shame on your family?" My heart was thudding violently. I cut some pie and thrust it towards him, keeping busy, not trusting myself to understand what he was trying to say.

"There would be no shame; my parents would welcome you. It would bring such happiness to our family. Everything has changed now."

"Changed?"

"It's Nathan..." His head was lowered, in his hands now, tufts of red-brown hair sprouted through his fingers. Then, head and eyes were raised a little as Thomas forced himself to tell me: "There was an accident and he was killed, just six weeks ago."

"Nathan?" I stopped trying to avoid him; he had all

my attention.

"It was all so foolish, you know Nathan..." The words came in a rush. "He jumped a dyke, there was no need for it, but that was Nathan – a risk-taker. The horse stumbled and fell, and that was it. There was a bridge nearby, but he did have to jump, didn't he? Nathan had to fool around."

"I'm so sorry." My hand reached across and he took it. "I liked him, he was fun, irritating sometimes, but I liked him."

"He liked to tease you." There was a hint of a smile now at the shared memories. "Let you think I was to marry Abigail, do you remember her? I was angry with him about that, messing around as usual. He had grown up a bit recently though and was thinking of marriage himself."

"Your parents, how are they?"

"Tired, you'll find they've aged, if... if you come back."

"I've made a life for myself here now." I took my hand from his and concentrated on my drink for a moment. "I never stopped loving you but so much has happened and maybe we can't go back."

"We can't go back, but I have regretted how we parted. I should have never allowed it. If you've any feelings left for me then we should grasp this chance of happiness."

"It will be a different place with both Nathan and Jess gone..."

It was Eliza who told Mother and myself about Jessica. Her mother had died last summer, days after her stillborn son. Kate was a decent woman and well liked. A fine needlewoman, good housewife and mother. It was very sad, but it seemed that the family were coping.

Then, Eliza told us – in a cruel gossipy way, which made me feel sick to the core – of how Jessica's body had been found lying in a shallow dyke. It was at the end of the summer; Isaac had been checking the sheep when he found her, and it was clear that this was no accident. It was Farmer Farley and Isaac who removed the body and had the dreadful task of telling her father and brother.

Within hours the whispered rumours had begun and Eliza repeated them with relish. While the villagers reeled from the shock, they learnt that Jessica's stomach was excessively bloated and it was clear that she was expecting a child.

Poor Jessica; how desperate she must have been to take her own life. I couldn't stop thinking of her alone, with no one to confide in, or advise her. I wished I had been closer; perhaps I could have helped. That it should be Jessica in this situation was unbelievable. A quiet, serious, respectable, God-fearing young woman, who would do nothing to cause shame on her parents.

"Eliza told me... about Jess."

"She lies on our land, to the east of the churchyard, as close to the graves of her family as possible."

"She couldn't be in the church grounds, I know." My hands were in his and for a moment we sat in silence, thinking of the deaths of two young people.

"Did you hear about the funeral? What her father did?"

"Eliza said nothing of the funeral."

"It was brave of him; he stood up and told us all that we need not point our fingers at local men and suspect them of doing wrong by his daughter." His fingers tightened around mine. "You know what I mean, Anna? That she was..."

"I know."

"Clement Browning stood there and said that there had been mention of a man who was not from this area and he was the one who had caused dishonour to the family, leading his daughter to despair." Thomas looked beyond me, his eyes unfocused, seeing the scene unfold. "Of course, there was still gossip, but people were relieved that their sons, brothers and husbands were not under suspicion."

"You tell it better than Eliza did; you care about people and I love you for it."

"You love me?" his eyes lit up, a cautious smile growing.

"I mean… I never stopped, but it doesn't mean..."

"I know. I hurt you. But I can hope?"

"I think so."

His smile was cautious at first, then it spread until his eyes, which were fixed on mine, creased at the corners and the joy shone from them. It was infectious; I let myself relax and returned the smile.

"You don't know how much I missed you." A hint of his smile remained, but Thomas was more serious now.

"The same as I missed you."

"I know and I hurt you, and I don't know if I can ever make it up to you."

"We've wasted enough time with our regrets." I gathered our cups and plates, taking them to the sink.

"So, you might come home?" He pushed back his chair and stood, filling the room with his height and presence.

"You know, I never dared to hope…" I turned and he was right behind me.

"Well you can… we can." He gently pushed back

stray strands of my hair, his fingers a little rough on my cheeks and then my neck. "Come home and marry me, Anna."

"I'm afraid to go back, but if I don't?"

"So you will?" His hand still played with my hair; our eyes were locked together.

"I will."

Thomas pulled me closer and we kissed gently, then he paused, his eyes questioning. I gave a slight smile and again we kissed, more deeply this time. He had returned for me. For three years I had been tormented by recurring dreams of Thomas and me being together again at last, only to wake and relive the rejection and loneliness. This was real; it had to be. We parted slightly.

"Mother..."

"I know. We need to talk to her – will she be disappointed?"

"Perhaps at first, but she wants me to be happy."

"She'll miss you." Thomas went to the door and looked out into the yard and up at the grey winter sky. "It's been three years but already I have to leave you again; it's a two-hour journey."

"When will you... what will?" I was still wary of being too hopeful.

"I'll return next week, on the Sunday, and if that is too soon I'll return every week until you are ready to come with me." With one long stride he was close to me again, both my hands in his. "Come back with me, see my parents and you will know you are welcome. Shall I speak with your mother?"

"No, I shall talk to her and Aunt Emm."

"Tell her that you can stay with us and we will marry as soon as you like. She knows my family; she can be sure that you will be safe and well cared for.

They would be so pleased if I could tell them that you will be with us soon."

"Come then, you should leave so as to be home by dusk, and I'll talk with Mother today."

"And next week…?"

"If all is well, we'll be together."

We returned to the bar, our tightly held hands only releasing at the last moment. Aunt Emm made a show of being busy, while Mother stood and scanned both of our faces, needing some answers.

"Thank you for letting me have some time with Anna, Mistress Smith."

"And will you be returning?"

"I will."

"I see."

I noticed that, beyond my mother, Michael still sat at his usual table. He had been looking towards us, but turned away to avoid my glance. He exchanged a few words with his brother and both men left in silence. I felt a pang of guilt for he clearly had some affection for me and only that afternoon I had encouraged him. Mother turned to watch their departing backs and shook her head slightly, disappointment showing as she faced us again.

"I don't want to lose my daughter, Thomas. But I want her to be happy."

"That's all I want." His hand took mine. Mother saw but it told her nothing that she did not already know. "I have to go home now, before night falls. Anna will speak with you, and I hope that I will be welcome when I return next week."

"If Anna is happy, then you are welcome. Safe journey home and send my best wishes to your family."

"I will."

Reluctantly, we parted and I followed Thomas to the door. I watched him mount his horse; he bent down and kissed me lightly on the cheek before turning in the direction of his home. I waited until he was out of sight, then stood a little longer, not looking at anything in particular but not wanting to break the spell of the moment.

Anna's Story
Part Two
Chapter Two

Over the next few days, I started to pack my belongings. There were personal things: a few books, pens and a decorative wooden box that held some beads, brooches and hair-clips. I opened this box and took out my treasures one at a time, holding them to the light, looking at the detail and the changing colours of the glass beads. Each piece had a story – it was a present from my mother, maybe a Christmas gift from my father or a birthday present from Jessica. Perhaps I had chosen it from a pedlar at a country fair, here in Appledore.

In a small velvet bag, unopened for years, was a ring. I saved this until last. Carefully I took it out and held the gold circlet up to the light, twisting it one way, then another, following the simple engraved pattern. Thomas had said that we would marry, and I wanted him to be the one to put it on my finger again.

"Are you going to wear it?" I had barely noticed my mother coming into the small room we shared.

"Not yet, but soon I hope." Reluctantly I replaced the ring in its bag and pulled the drawstrings tight.

"You'll be well cared for by the Farley family. We must put the past behind us; they did what they had to do to save the farm. I couldn't wish for better for you, except…"

"I know you had hopes for Michael, but he would always be second best."

"I see that now, and I know you'll be happy with Thomas. I just wish that we were closer."

"It's not so far and you're settled here with Aunt Emm, but if you wanted…"

"No Anna. I would not return to Hope." Mother turned and from the bottom of her wooden chest she pulled out a package, wrapped in cloth. "I saved this for you, just in case…"

I knew what it was before I carefully unfolded the layers of cloth, but in three years I had never thought of my wedding dress and what had become of it. The heavy pale green silk was a luxury, given to me by my father a few months before he left. It was not the type of gift that a blacksmith bought for his daughter; it was a gift from a man who had organised a group of smugglers. The silk would have been destined for a fine lady of rank and fortune.

I held up the dress. We had copied all we knew of the latest fashions when Mother and I had painstakingly stitched night after night in the weeks preceding the wedding that never happened. It was frivolous, for it really was too fancy to be worn again, but perhaps could be altered afterwards. The neckline was square and from the shoulders hung long sleeves which widened at the bottom and ended in a point. The low waistline echoed the point and the skirt then fell in folds to the ground. We had carefully embroidered around the hems and neckline.

"I'd forgotten how beautiful it was," I carefully lowered it on to my bed and examined the delicate stitching.

"We did a fine job on it. Pack it away for now and you can ask Mistress Farley if she has a safe place to hang it." Mother started carefully folding the dress, stopping to admire a detail here and there. She paused, "Oh, I nearly forgot why I came looking for you. Emm was asking if you would mind going along to the chandlers; we'll be needing more candles within the next day or so."

"I'll go in a moment." I turned and made a show of checking over my special possessions again.

"There's plenty of time to pack up your things."

"I know... I just..."

"You might see Michael in the village. It wouldn't do any harm to say goodbye to him."

"I shouldn't avoid him. Michael deserves an apology; I know that." I reached for my cloak.

"Men are proud and no doubt he is feeling sore. I'm sure that he would rather speak with you in private than in front of the whole village, as you're sure to see him in church on Sunday."

"I'll go now then and it's likely that I won't see him. But if I do, then I can hope to leave with no ill feeling."

With my basket swinging beside me, I set out for the village shops. In a few days' time I would have a longer walk in to the town if I wanted to buy anything. Of course the farm would provide many of the necessities, but it was nice to have local shops and the opportunity to meet people and pause for a talk.

There had been some rain recently, causing the road to be wet and slippery in places. I carefully picked my way over some rough ground and looking up, found myself almost walking into Michael as he stepped out of a roadside cottage.

"Good morning, Anna."

"Good morning." Surprised, I found myself

colouring. "It's a pleasant day." I couldn't think of what to say and when I spoke it sounded foolish.

"I didn't come for you last Sunday as we arranged… for the walk."

"No… I"

"Things have changed, I know, and I hope you'll be happy." He stood, looking straight into my face, holding my gaze.

"I never expected… never thought I would see him again." I tried to keep my eyes on his, but my hands nervously twisted my basket round and round.

"I know that, and if he had to come for you, best he did it now."

"I'm sorry."

"Well, be happy." Michael smiled briefly and turned away.

"Thank you, and you too." I continued on my way, relieved now that I had seen him. Mother was right, he was a good man, but he wasn't Thomas.

Thomas was expected any minute. The weather was dull; a blanket of cloud covered every part of the sky. It gave no reason to hinder a journey though. I tried to keep myself busy, but flitted from one task to another, never far from a window or door. Although the wait seemed unbearable, he arrived in good time.

I was at the door before he had climbed down from the small farm cart. My heart raced as I gazed up at him, speechless for a moment, hardly believing that this time had come.

"I came as soon as I could. You didn't doubt me?" Thomas' smile was wide.

"No, I …" my words were muffled as I was enveloped in his arms, my head against his shoulders, the rough cloth of his cloak against my cheek.

"I love you, Anna, and today you come home to me." He kissed me lightly on top of my head and then withdrew. "I should see your mother and aunt; this will be hard for them."

"It will be hard for all three of us, but you and I are to be together and in time they'll accept it."

I led him in to the kitchen. Aunt Emm had been busy making hot drinks and cutting chunks of gingerbread. My mother was packing some bread and cold meat for the journey.

"Sit yourself down, Thomas. You must need warming through after being on the road for hours." Aunt Emm pushed a warm rosemary drink towards him and the largest piece of gingerbread.

"I made good time, and have blankets to keep Anna warm." He turned to my aunt when he spoke, but we couldn't take our eyes off each other for long.

"How are your parents?" Mother sat down, placing the food package on the table. "Anna told us about Nathan. I'm so sorry; how you must all be hurting."

"They're coping, but Father tires more easily now and Mother struggles to accept he's gone."

"There will be some changes for Anna."

"Aye, more people have left Hope, there is less sense of community, but we try to enjoy the seasonal celebrations as we always have done."

"Christmas, Harvest time and of course Midsummer's Eve. We had some good times and your mother knew how to put on a good feast for us." Mother looked into the distance and smiled at the memories. We'd spent too long remembering the bad ones since we left. "Old John with his fiddle and Sara playing the whistle; didn't the young ones love to dance?"

"There will be a wedding soon and I hope you'll

both come. Anna is welcome at Hope and you are too; the past is all behind us and everyone knows that you did not benefit from…"

"Thank you, Thomas. We'll be there."

Thomas turned to me, "I know the spring or summer would perhaps be nicer, but so long to wait. Would January be too soon?"

"We've wasted too much time. It sounds perfect." I couldn't stop the smile from spreading all over my face.

"We'll wrap up warm and your garland shall be evergreen leaves with winter berries," Mother enthused. "Just a small gathering… what with all that has happened."

"Aye, it sounds perfect," agreed Thomas. Then thinking of recent tragedies, his face dropped.

"It will be lovely," I told him and squeezed his hand gently.

Our drinks and gingerbread were finished; the conversation dried up. Thomas and I had a long journey ahead of us, but first were the goodbyes that we dreaded. We all knew that the time had come, but were reluctant to be the one to suggest it was time to leave. It was Aunt Emm who stood and voiced our thoughts.

"We don't want Anna to leave, and of course she doesn't want to leave us, but she wants to be with Thomas. It'll be dark in no time, so best you two are on your way."

"Of course," Mother picked up one of my bags from the pile on the kitchen floor, then led the way to the yard where the horse and cart waited patiently. "We want to know that you'll be in the warm and dry before darkness falls and it's a relief to know you'll not be with strangers."

We followed her, each with a bag or package. They were safely stowed in the back of the cart and under the seat. Our eyes were bright with tears as I exchanged the final hugs with my mother and aunt. There were few words left to say. Thomas stepped up into the cart and reached down to offer his hand to help me up.

"Have a good journey, and be happy," Mother said. At her side my aunt nodded her agreement.

"You know she'll be well cared for. We'll say goodbye for now, but meet again soon." Thomas gathered the reins and the horse began to walk on.

"Goodbye Mother, goodbye Aunt Emm. God bless."

"God save you, Anna."

We didn't speak much for the first few miles; the occasional tear rolled down my face. Thomas held my hand and I was happy, far happier than I ever hoped to be. For now there would still be a few tears and I knew that Thomas understood.

It was dusk when we turned the corner to see Hope before us with the tiny church and parson's house to our left and the remainder of cottages on my right. There was no yellow-pink light from the last of the sun, just a gradual darkening of the grey sky. The dew was starting to form and the blanket in which I was wrapped felt damp to touch, but within it, I was still warm.

Shutters and curtains were closed in those few cottages that were still inhabited. Only the cracks of light showing at windows and the occasional bleating of the sheep told us that the place was not entirely deserted. I knew that there had been some changes and most of the cottages were now ruined.

We passed the forge and adjoining cottage, now

derelict and unwanted. Only the sockets of the windows remained. Weeds grew in abundance, spilling into our old home, battling to cling on to any suitable crevice. The roof had surrendered to the weeds and the weather; the thatch was sparse on one side and there seemed to be an area where the roof timbers had fallen in.

"I'm sorry. What a miserable way to return." Thomas put an arm round my waist and gently kissed my cheek. "It'll look better in the morning."

"I knew there were changes; I should have been prepared."

"It's been a long journey."

"You're right; it will be better in the morning."

To my left, the parsonage was, according to Thomas, the exception, having been repaired recently. The stone, thatch and timber had been taken from neighbouring cottages, leaving no hope that they might be restored. I strained my eyes, but it was farther back from the road, and looked no different in the failing light. Standing on its mound was the tiny church. I wondered if it had benefited from some repairs, but suspected that it still suffered from damp and wood rot. Whatever its condition, it was our church and the local people would patch, repair and decorate, as best they could.

Opposite the church were the remains of a pretty terrace of cottages. Their upper windows once peeped through the thatch; now their frames were broken and fallen in. One had been derelict for some time, and in the past few years the decay had increased so only a weed-infested shell remained. The middle cottage had been the home of John and Mary, with his elderly mother. They had recently left to live with their daughter in Dymchurch.

It was the next cottage that caused the greatest pain for me. It was a house full of happy memories from my childhood. The Browning family had welcomed me into their home as I grew up and became good friends with Jessica. They were kindly, decent people, well liked by everyone. According to Thomas, the cottage would still make a suitable home for a family but no one wanted it; not caring to live where there has been so much sorrow. Instead they took the stone, thatch, windows – anything that would make good another house or help towards building a new cottage.

"Are you nervous?" Thomas turned the horse towards the farm track.

"Nervous?" I considered the question for a moment. "No, but a little shy… it has been a long time."

"I'm sorry. It was too long."

"It doesn't matter any more."

The lookers' cottages were to our left. Smoke from the chimneys, light at the windows and the sounds of children playing brought a smile to my face. At least here in this place there was still life and activity. They looked to be in good condition, too; there would always be work on the farm and labourers needed homes.

Finally, we turned into the farmyard. Barns and farm buildings were on either side of us. Although it was too dark to see inside them, I could hear the sounds of animals. The horse stopped and I knew that she would welcome her bed and feed.

My attention was now on the farmhouse. It was a fine house; the red brick gave it warmth, even on this dull evening. The windows had lots of tiny pieces of glass held by diamond shaped frames of wood and metal. Mistress Farley was fond of flowers and although her display was over for this year, the bare branches of a rose bush reached upwards and clung to the wall around the front door. The roof was tiled, which was unusual as most people used thatch for their homes. Smoke spiralled from the high chimneys; within minutes I would be warming myself beside that fire.

I knew how it would be inside. Farmer Farley relaxing in his chair beside the fire, but he was never idle. There would be something in his hands, perhaps a tool that needed repair or a piece of wood to be whittled, until it became a bowl or a spoon. I expected his smile to be wide and welcoming and there to be some questions about our journey and my life in Appledore, but not too much – leave all the gossip to the women!

Some light showed at the kitchen window; it was the heart of the home. I had known the family long enough to know that a warm meal awaited us. The great scrubbed table may have the remains of the day's activities on it and these would be pushed aside to make way for the important business of eating a nourishing supper. Mistress Farley would be telling me the news of the area, whilst cooking, setting the table, tidying up and perhaps caring for an orphan animal, all at the same time.

Ellen was now a young woman of fifteen years. As a child she had been lively, friendly and confident. I expected her to have matured, but I hoped to find her much the same as she always was. Ellen was a child when I left, now we could be friends – sisters. I was sure that she would be good company.

"I'll take the horse, shall I?" The voice came from the darkness.

"Robert, thank you. Has all been well today?" Thomas began to climb down from the cart.

"It has, Mr Farley, and I repaired those fences." I saw him then, but of course I knew the voice for I had known Robert-the-looker all my life. He lived with his wife in one of the cottages set beside the farm track. He offered his hand: "Welcome home, Anna."

"Thank you." I accepted his hand and climbed down. "Is Isabel well?"

"She is, and no doubt she'll want to see you tomorrow." Robert reached in for my bags and placed them on the ground. "I'll put the horse away and be off home myself. Goodnight."

"Goodnight," we echoed.

We stood for a moment, watching Robert lead the horse and cart away before turning towards the house. Thomas took some of my bags in one hand and held out the other to me. I took it and held on tightly, in some ways not wanting this time alone with him to end, but it was cold, damp and becoming increasingly dark. A few steps away, the farmhouse and my new family waited for me.

"Are you ready?" He gave my hand a reassuring squeeze.

Looking into his face, I felt a surge of love and trust: "I am."

He opened the heavy front door and, hand in hand, we stepped into the warmth. Everyone was there, immediately turning from their tasks and with welcoming smiles they began to gather around.

"Here we are, back at last," Thomas said as his father gave him a friendly slap on the back and I found myself engulfed in the arms of his mother.

I was home.

Anna's Story
Part Two
Chapter Three

"It's a beautiful day, Anna." Ellen wiped away the water droplets from the bedroom window and looked from the back of the farmhouse across the fields. "Look at how blue the sky is; it could easily have been dull and misty."

"It wouldn't really matter." I smoothed the silk of my wedding dress, looking forward to wearing it later, before joining her at the window.

"I'm so pleased you came home and I have your company. The wedding gives us all something good to think about."

Ellen was thinking of Nathan, of course. I believed we all still expected him to be here, to appear suddenly and say it was all a joke, a game. It helped to have something to plan, to occupy us in the long winter evenings, something positive.

"It's wonderful to be home." I saw Thomas then, striding out across the field, and smiled to myself.

Our wedding day had come and it was going to be special. A time to celebrate, to enjoy ourselves and be grateful for what we had that day. No one could put aside all thoughts of the tragedies we had suffered in the last year. Terrible, unnecessary losses to both our family and the small community. There was sadness amongst the joy and out of respect for this the celebration would be small.

The day was well planned, with the routine farm chores to be done by the lookers and their wives. This left the family free to prepare the wedding feast. It was still early when Ellen and I came downstairs, but there was plenty of activity. Mother and Aunt Emm had arrived the evening before and were eager to help wherever they could.

"If you could stir the porridge, Eve... Martin will be in any moment. He promised he would not be getting mucky with the animals this morning." Mistress Farley checked on the pig that was roasting on the spit and added another log to the fire. "And Emm, if you could fetch the bowls, in the cupboard...that's it...what a help you both are!" Then, turning to note my arrival: "There she is... sit yourself down, Anna."

Mother ladled porridge into the bowls provided. "The weather looks to be fine," she said. "It's going to be a lovely day for your wedding."

"It will be perfect." The porridge was steaming; I added milk and stirred it. "Did you sleep well?"

"Very well; nice and comfortable." Mother and Aunt Emm had slept in Thomas' room, soon to be my room too.

"I wonder if Thomas slept so well." Aunt Emm sat down beside me. He had stayed with Robert and Isabel; I wouldn't see him until we were at the church.

The door flung open and Farmer Farley staggered in backwards. He carried one end of a table with Isaac at the other. They placed it against a wall; his wife nodded her approval.

"Some porridge, Martin?" asked my mother.

"Thank you, if you could ladle some out for me.

There are a few chairs and a bench to come in and I'll be finished for now."

"The pantry's full of food; I've been baking for days. Magota promised to bring cream, butter and milk from the dairy and I've got the cheese. Eve and Emm will help me lay it out on the table; it won't take long. Martin will set out the ale and wine over there, on the other table. Ellen, you'll see to the flowers. Anna will be wanting some brought in for her hair, and I know you girls will enjoy that." Mistress Farley was satisfied and sat down for her own breakfast.

"It's all arranged very nicely." Mother concluded, "Now I'll help tidy these dishes away."

"It's beautiful, Ellen." I held the wedding garland up and turning it one way, then another, admired the shiny darkness of the evergreen leaves, delicate winter berries and traditional rosemary.

"It's not the best time of year...."

"I love it, thank you. I think we're ready. Shall we go?"

Together we walked down the stairs; careful not to catch our dresses and holding them up to avoid collecting any dust. Ellen wore a dark green dress with velvet trims; it suited her very well. In her long, thick, red hair she wore a posy of berries and leaves, tied with a ribbon of the same green velvet.

I loved the pale green silk of my dress. My hair was loose, hanging straight down my back for the last time. A small enamelled pendant hung from a ribbon around my neck and on my right hand was my betrothal ring, which Thomas had placed on my finger that first evening we returned to Hope.

Stepping in to the kitchen we found that only Mistress Farley was there. She was dressed in her best Sunday skirt and bodice, a lace shawl in her hands.

"Well, don't you two look lovely? This is a good day for our family."

I gave her a quick hug, to let her know that I understood. Alongside her joy, there was sadness.

"Do I hear my sister has arrived?" I walked to the window.

"She has, your mother and aunt went to greet them. They are looking forward to seeing the little girls of course." Mistress Farley gave a last look at the feast laid out on the table, wrapped her shawl around her shoulders and asked: "Shall we go then?"

In the yard, Bess and Dolly, now aged five and three, ran around chasing each other. Their skirts were already muddied at the hem; their posies cast aside as they soon became a hindrance to their games. Eliza, a hand on her swollen stomach, leant heavily on her husband, William. It was my mother and aunt who tried in vain to calm the children down and interest them in something other than a game that was bound to end in a tearful mess.

William looked uncomfortable as he tried to keep his balance and keep hold of the girls' posies and cloaks. William and Eliza were accompanied by a pleasant young man. He was a little stocky, with fair hair, merry eyes and dimples that appeared frequently. Bertie worked alongside William at the forge as his apprentice. He would often come to the farm to buy dairy produce and always seemed to be in good spirits. I suspected that he had an interest in Ellen and noted that his gaze rested on her.

"Here she is then; Anna will do us all proud!" Eliza straightened herself and waddled over to admire my dress. "Very nice, I must say."

There were murmurs of agreement from everyone. Bess and Dolly forgot their games and ran over reluctantly to have their hands wiped by my mother before the dress was touched.

We started to walk across the yard but were all stopped by Eliza loudly voicing her demands.

"You go on, don't mind me, but I'm bursting to use the privy. William can wait for me, if Mother doesn't mind taking the girls, but watch them... little rascals. Round the back is it, Mistress Farley?"

Mistress Farley gave directions and our little group set off again. It was a beautiful morning, not too cold and the sky remained a clear blue. We reached the lookers' cottages and found that the men were already outside, waiting to join the small procession. Bertie produced a battered whistle and his joyful tunes had us humming along. Bess and Dolly were now joined by young Nicholas and Zachary; they danced along the grass verge.

As we turned on to the main road, we were greeted by relations of the Farley family, who clapped and cheered to see us coming. Ellen gave posies from the basket she carried. People were talking, laughing, telling the latest news, but I looked across the field to the tiny church. My eyes were on Thomas, as he stood with his father at the doorway, waiting for me. Although he was some distance away, I knew that he was looking at me too.

My heart lurched, as it still did, even though we had known each other for so long. Sometimes I would look out of a window and see him at work on the fields. Sometimes he would appear with dirt and animal feed on his clothes, his face, even his hair. Sometimes we would just be sitting down to a meal together and our eyes would meet, my heart would soar and I felt just as I did all those years ago when I was young and falling in love with him. I smiled; he couldn't see the smile, but for a moment it was as if it were just Thomas and me.

"You'll be married soon enough." Thomas' cousin, Lucy, had a lovely smile that lit up her eyes; she looked towards her husband and first child. "I hope you'll be as happy as we are. I know you will."

"Thank you. I know we will."

"And do I sense another romance? Ellen is growing up."

"She is, and anyone would be lucky to have her." I looked towards Ellen and Bertie; he held her basket whilst she put a posy in Dolly's hair. "He seems to be a decent young man."

"Today is your day. Let's not keep Thomas waiting any longer."

Bertie's whistle started again, to be joined by Andrew Farley, brother to Lucy. Sometimes their melodies were as one, often they became disjointed, but they were merry and we were all caught up in the tune. So, we were a cheerful group as we crossed the dyke and took the last steps along the track to the church.

Thomas stood, perhaps a little uncomfortable in his new suit of good cloth and polished leather boots. His father was beside him, his cheeks hollow and body appearing more frail than it had been three years before. It was now more noticeable that Thomas stood a little taller than the older man. His red hair shone in the sunshine, a contrast to his father's, now totally grey.

"Doesn't she look beautiful, Father?" Thomas took a step towards me and took my hand, our fingers linked.

"She does. Anna will make you proud." Farmer Farley gave his son a pat on the shoulder, then turned to ask: "Parson, shall we go in?"

The parson led the way and we followed through the ornamental archway, our hands held tightly. The guests followed behind and settled down to enjoy the service. As their eyes adjusted to the dim light they commented on the pretty displays of berries and leaves. Dried lavender and scented petals attempted to cover the ever-present smells of decaying wood and damp stone. The sunlight filtered through both the tiny, high windows and the holes in the roof.

"Shove up, William. I'm not sitting in a puddle, not for my sister's wedding." Even in church, Eliza said what needed to be said, never lowering her voice or thinking of other people's feelings.

William found himself squashed against the cold, damp stone wall. Dolly was on his lap; she leant forwards, trying to pull at the clips in Aunt Emm's hair. William remained as quiet and gentle as he had been on his own wedding day.

Eliza turned one way, then another, trying to make herself more comfortable on the hard narrow pew. Leaning forward, she jabbed at our mother. "Good to see our Anna getting married, no one wants to be an old maid."

"It is." Mother spoke quietly, not wanting to be involved with any disruption. It had been hard for her to return to Hope, but she had been made welcome and was relaxing now. She too had aged in the past few years, her hair now a mixture of silver and gold and her face showing deep lines. I admired her determination to be there for my wedding. Bess sat perched between my mother and aunt, enjoying the attention as they whispered to her.

"Well, I hope they hurry up. I can't abide these hard seats and there's sure to be a good spread back at the farmhouse." Again, Eliza moved her great body and hitched one swollen ankle over the other; stained shift and tatty stockings were clear for all to see.

They were the sole members of my family. Thomas' immediate family sat behind him. Then there was Thomas' uncle with his wife, grown up children and their families. The lookers and regular farm labourers gathered at the back. We made a modest group for a wedding but it was not practical for people to travel during the winter.

Old John, parson's assistant and part-time labourer, came to a shaky end of the tune he played on his fiddle. An expectant silence fell on the congregation and the parson invited us to start with a prayer.

Then the time came. With our fingers entwined and our eyes only for each other, Thomas and I made our wedding vows. We stood on the very spot where we had been betrothed in the winter of 1586. Now, three years later, the gold band Thomas gave me was changed from my right to my left hand. We were pronounced man and wife and as we kissed, there was a cheer from the back of the church, followed by much clapping! We smiled a little shyly, not used to the attention.

The two of us led the way out from the church, family and friends poured along behind. They threw grains of rice that found their way into my bodice and down my back. We were congratulated and thanked people for coming. All the time Thomas stood by my side and I was filled with a warm feeling of happiness. Looking up into his face I could see my feelings reflected.

"I'd like to thank the parson for the service." Farmer Farley stepped up on to a mound of fallen stone. His voice was raised and he gained everyone's attention for a moment. "You are all welcome back at the house to help us continue celebrating the marriage of my son, Thomas, to Anna."

"Well, let's go then," Eliza began to waddle down the path, her arm linked through her husband's, pulling him firmly to her side.

"The girls..." William looked back helplessly.

"Mother will mind them; she's having a lovely time fussing over them."

Our guests were ushered into the farmhouse, not inclined to dawdle with a cosy room and a table laden with food before them. The fire had been smouldering and leapt into life as more wood was added. Shawls and cloaks were discarded, and as people warmed themselves by the fire, they praised the decorations and fine feast.

"Now, if Eve will help me, let's all get a nice cup of spiced wine to cheer ourselves." Mistress Farley took the great pan of hot, scented liquid from beside the fire and ladled it into cups that my mother held up for her.

All the company made themselves comfortable: on a chair, a stool, or squeezed next to another body on a bench. The children were content to sit on a rug. They talked non-stop – about the service, family news or local gossip. Wooden plates were piled high with food and soon everyone was well fed and content. Thomas and I were barely able to exchange a few words before someone else had to congratulate us, pass on some local news or encourage us to taste a piece of pie, gingerbread or an almond sweet. But there was no need for words, we knew how happy we were and would have time for each other later. Often, our eyes would meet or our hands would join and silent messages of love and understanding were exchanged.

"Do you think he likes my dress, that it isn't too fancy?" Ellen sat beside me, carefully smoothing the dark green velvet.

"He?" I teased, knowing the answer.

"Bertie. You do like him, don't you? Do you think that he notices me?"

"He has eyes for no one else; he is looking towards you now."

"I shan't look back; he'll know we're talking about him."

"The dress is lovely, and the colour is perfect with your red hair. It is fancy of course, but isn't a wedding a special day?"

"Will Father approve?"

"Bertie's learning a trade and is a good-natured, respectable young man. I'm sure that you needn't worry." I looked towards him again and, catching my eye, he made his way towards us.

"I must congratulate you, I am sure you will both be very happy." Bertie's smile was wide, dimples appearing.

"Thank you, Bertie. I'm glad you came. I see my husband is trying to get my attention; I'll leave Ellen to look after you."

Looking back, I saw them laughing together and wondered if it was too soon to be planning a summer betrothal, or even a wedding. The chatter became quieter now as the warmth and wine relaxed us. Only the children called out and laughed with the same energy. The fire was left to smoulder and the great wooden table no longer groaned under the weight of our feast.

Farmer Farley was talking with the parson. Eventually he moved away, leaving the churchman to have food pressed upon him by Mistress Farley and my mother. Pulling up a stool beside Thomas and myself, Thomas' father relayed the latest news.

"It seems as if this could be the last wedding at Hope," he reported.

"The last wedding?" I repeated with surprise.

"The parson has just been telling me that he has been asked to become the rector of St Nicholas. He'll be moving to New Romney. Our community is too small; there's no money to repair the church or parsonage. So, you see, this may be the last wedding. It seems that we'll walk to the town to worship."

"It's a good move for the parson," Thomas reflected.

"Of course, he is a young man still, with energy to devote to his flock; he deserves to have more people listening to his sermons."

"How sad that our community has become so small that we can't support our parson." My thoughts were still on our wedding service and I was thankful that we had been able to marry there. My hand sought Thomas' and he squeezed it gently.

The news travelled swiftly, and when Eliza waddled over it was the topic of her conversation. "I hear we're havin' a new rector in Romney, what with everyone leaving Hope. They keep on marrying or dying and it's only the Farleys left now."

"He takes a good service," Mr Farley commented.

"Oh aye, I know he does." A marzipan sweet was stuffed into her mouth; Eliza licked her bulbous lips with relish. "You'll have a walk into town now on Sundays. That's all right while you're young, but not easy once you put on a bit of weight, if you know what I mean...."

"Bess and Dolly look as if they are enjoying themselves." Thomas looked over to them; the little girls were hiding beside a cupboard, then jumping out at Zachary.

"Aye, nice bit of food, someone to play with, they're fine. I was saying, about everyone leaving – William has been thinking about taking the business into New Romney."

"Close the forge?" That would be something else changed; another link with my childhood gone.

"Move it, not close it. I told him there's not much work out here; the farmers will be just as happy to come into town, and he'll be close by if I need him."

"I hear Eliza is telling you about the forge." We were joined by my mother. "We had some happy times there, but...."

"Some sad ones, too," my eyes met Mother's. "William and Eliza must do what is best for them."

"They must, and there will be more trade in the town." Then she added on a lighter note: "I came over to see if you were ready to cut the bride cake now?"

"That will suit me nicely, and then we'll be on our way." Eliza's gaze fell on the cake, which stood in pride of place on the centre of the table.

Thomas led the way and rapped on it with a wooden spoon. Everyone turned, and he had their attention. "My wife..." this was followed by cheers, "thank you... and I will cut the bride cake now."

We cut some slices to more cheers and clapping. Then Mistress Farley cut some more and placed them on a platter, which she offered to the guests.

The wedding party was coming to an end. Most people needed to travel home. In the summer-time, guests would have stayed until late in the evening, fulfilling all the long-standing traditions. The women would have prepared the bride for bed and the men would have brought the groom to join her. We were spared this ritual: the bawdy jokes, well-meant advice, sharing of ribbons amongst unmarried girls, the embarrassment.

The lookers and their families left; the men to work on the farm, the women to their homes. Farmer Farley's brother and his family wrapped up warmly for the walk back to Ivychurch. The parson and his family returned to his parsonage, perhaps to begin to prepare for his move to the town.

Finally Eliza, William and Bertie gathered the children and prepared to leave.

"Would you like some pie for your supper?" asked Mistress Farley. "We've plenty to spare."

"I won't say no to that." Eliza's beady eyes scanned the table of food: "Go nicely with a bit of cheese and pickled veg, that pie would."

"Of course."

Eliza snatched at the basket of food. "Off we go then, it's been a lovely day, and a good spread of food. Very nice indeed."

William and Bertie murmured their thanks and agreement.

"Sorry, we couldn't stay a bit longer Anna. Seems like we've missed out on some of the fun." Eliza turned as she waddled out of the door. "But, don't you worry, we decorated the bed with ribbons and corn – for luck, you know…."

When I woke the next morning, I was alone in Thomas' bed… in our bed. With a farm to look after, Thomas had risen as dawn broke. The air was chilly; I rose and wrapped a blanket around my shoulders. Pulling back the curtains, I wiped the window and peered out. There was our church, the mist slowly shifting around it. It had stood there for 400 years, but apparently we didn't need it any more; there weren't enough people to fill it. Our parson was wanted elsewhere.

Soon, when we worship we'll go to St Nicholas in New Romney. When our children are christened it will be at St Nicholas, and when they marry it will be at that great parish church. Our little church will crumble, for the decay is already setting in, and who will have the money or interest in repairing it?

In years to come people will pass by the ruins and perhaps wonder about those who once worshipped there. No one will know, no one will be able to tell, of the farmer and the girl who fell in love with him, and how happy they were.

THE END

About the Author

Romney Marsh writer, Emma Batten, loves to combine her interest in local history with creative writing. It is important to her that historical details are accurate in order to give readers an authentic insight into life on Romney Marsh. She enjoys giving author talks about her journey as a writer, planning unique writing workshops and meeting her local readers.

A Place Called Hope is Emma's first novel.

Books
Reading order and publication dates

The Dungeness Saga (also featuring Lydd and Ashford) set in late Victorian times through to WW2:

Still Shining Bright* (2020): Cora and her daughter, Emily, are brought ashore to Dungeness by lifeboat. With no home or possessions, they rely on the kindness of strangers, and Cora must use her wit to survive.

Reckless Choices* (2021): A chance meeting on a train upsets Emily, while on the streets of Ashford someone lurks waiting to make trouble. As tensions brew within a close family, the young woman makes a rash choice.

Secrets of the Shingle (2016 & 2020): A mystery set on the wild, windswept wastes of the Dungeness peninsula in the 19th century and seen through the eyes of a naive young teacher.

Stranger on the Point (2018): Lily sets off to discover the remote coastal village her mother called home. A wrong turning takes her to a place where her arrival brings hope. The story of a determined young woman's quest to fulfil her worth, as shadows of WW1 live on.

The Artist's Gift (2019): This tells the story of a fictional young woman, widowed through the war and living amongst real life events during the Second World War. Inspired by the bombing of Lydd Church.

*Prequels to *Secrets of the Shingle*

Stand-alone novels:

A Place Called Hope (2005, reworked 2019): Set in the 16th century, this tells the story of two young women living through the decline of a remote settlement named Hope on Romney Marsh.

But First Maintain the Wall (2019): Set in Georgian Dymchurch. Harry is passing through the village when the seawall breaches and events force him to stay. As an outsider, he struggles to be accepted and a tentative friendship is forged with a young woman who seeks answers to her past.

What the Monk Didn't See (2017 & 2021): The story of New Romney and the 1287 storm, which changed the fortunes of the town forever. As the storm breaks out, a monk climbs to the roof of the church tower. It is a superb vantage point, but what doesn't he see?

The Saxon Series introduces West Hythe, Lyminge and Aldington in 7th- century Anglo-Saxon times:

The Pendant Cross (2020): For a few days a year, the Sandtun (West Hythe) is used as a seasonal trading settlement. While they await the boats from Francia, friendships are made and hatred brews. Meanwhile four monks travel by night carrying a precious secret.

The Sacred Stone (2021): An earthquake uncovers a Roman altar buried in the foundations of an old fort. An ambitious thane and his priest are determined to secure this prize, and their actions have repercussions on the people of Aldington.

For more details take a look at Emma's website:
www.emmabattenauthor.com

Printed in Great Britain
by Amazon